Mr. Incoul's Mis

Edgar Saltus

Alpha Editions

This edition published in 2023

ISBN : 9789357951265

Design and Setting By
Alpha Editions
www.alphaedis.com
Email - info@alphaedis.com

Contents

CHAPTER I.
MR. INCOUL.

When Harmon Incoul's wife died, the world in which he lived said that he would not marry again. The bereavement which he had suffered was known to be bitter, and it was reported that he might betake himself to some foreign land. There was, for that matter, nothing to keep him at home. He was childless, his tastes were too simple to make it necessary for him to reside as he had, hitherto, in New York, and, moreover, he was a man whose wealth was proverbial. Had he so chosen, he had little else to do than to purchase a ticket and journey wheresoever he listed, and the knowledge of this ability may have been to him not without its consolations. Yet, if he attempted to map some plan, and think which spot he would prefer, he probably reflected that whatever place he might choose, he would, in the end, be not unlike the invalid who turns over in his bed, and then turns back again on finding the second position no better than the first. However fair another sky might be, it would not make his sorrow less acute.

He was then one of those men whose age is difficult to determine. He had married when quite young, and at the time of his widowerhood he must have been nearly forty, but years had treated him kindly. His hair, it is true, was inclined to scantiness, and his skin was etiolated, but he was not stout, his teeth were sound, he held himself well, and his eyes had not lost their lustre. At a distance, one might have thought him in the thirties, but in conversation his speech was so measured, and about his lips there was a compression such that the ordinary observer fancied him older than he really was.

His position was unexceptionable. He had inherited a mile of real estate in a populous part of New York, together with an accumulation of securities sufficient for the pay and maintenance of a small army. The foundations of this wealth had been laid by an ancestor, materially increased by his grandfather, and consolidated by his father, who had married a Miss Van Tromp, the ultimate descendant of the Dutch admiral.

His boyhood had not been happy. His father had been a lean, taciturn, unlovable man, rigid in principles, stern in manner, and unyielding in his adherence to the narrowest tenets of Presbyterianism. His mother had died while he was yet in the nursery, and, in the absence of any softening influence, the angles of his earliest nature were left in the rough.

At school, he manifested a vindictiveness of disposition which made him feared and disliked. One day, a comrade raised the lid of a desk adjoining his own. The raising of the lid was abrupt and possibly intentional. It jarred him in a task. The boy was dragged from him senseless and bleeding. In college, he became aggrieved at a tutor. For three weeks he had him shadowed, then, having discovered an irregularity in his private life, he caused to be laid before the faculty sufficient evidence to insure his removal. Meanwhile, acting presumably on the principle that an avowed hatred is powerless, he treated the tutor as though the grievance had been forgotten. A little later, owing to some act of riotous insubordination, he was himself expelled, and the expulsion seemed to have done him good. He went to Paris and listened decorously to lectures at the Sorbonne, after which he strayed to Heidelberg, where he sat out five semesters without fighting a duel or making himself ill with beer. In his fourth summer abroad, he met the young lady who became his wife. His father died, he returned to New York, and thereafter led a model existence.

He was proud of his wife and indulgent to her every wish. During the years that they lived together, there was no sign or rumor of the slightest disagreement. She was of a sweet and benevolent disposition, and though beyond a furtive coin he gave little to the poor, he encouraged her to donate liberally to the charities which she was solicited to assist. She was a woman with a quick sense of the beautiful, and in spite of the simplicity of his own tastes, he had a house on Madison avenue rebuilt and furnished in such a fashion that it was pointed out to strangers as one of the chief palaces of the city. She liked, moreover, to have her friends about her, and while he cared as much for society as he did for the negro minstrels, he insisted that she should give entertainments and fill the house with guests. In the winter succeeding the fifteenth anniversary of their marriage, Mrs. Incoul caught a chill, took to her bed and died, forty-eight hours later, of pneumonia.

It was then that the world said that he would not marry again. For two years he gave the world no reason to say otherwise, and for two years time hung heavy on his hands. He was an excellent chess-player, and interested in archæological pursuits, but beyond that his resources were limited. He was too energetic to be a dilettante, he had no taste for horseflesh, the game of speculation did not interest him, and his artistic tendencies were few. Now and then, a Mr. Blydenburg, a florid, talkative man, a widower like himself, came to him of an evening, and the chess-board was prepared. But practically his life was one of solitude, and the solitude grew irksome to him.

Meanwhile his wound healed as wounds do. The cicatrix perhaps was ineffaceable, but at least the smart had subsided, and in its subsidence he found that the great house in which he lived had taken on the silence of a tomb. Soon he began to go out a little. He was seen at meetings of the Archæological Society and of an afternoon he was visible in the Park. He even attended a reception given to an English thinker, and one night applauded Salvini.

At first he went about with something of that uncertainty which visits one who passes from a dark room to a bright one, but in a little while his early constraint fell from him, and he found that he could mingle again with his fellows.

At some entertainment he met a delicious young girl, Miss Maida Barhyte by name, whom for the moment he admired impersonally, as he might have admired a flower, and until he saw her again, forgot her very existence. It so happened, however, that he saw her frequently. One evening he sat next to her at a dinner and learning from her that she was to be present at a certain reception, made a point of being present himself.

This reception was given by Mrs. Bachelor, a lady, well known in society, who kept an unrevised list, and at stated intervals issued invitations to the dead, divorced and defaulted. When she threw her house open, she liked to have it filled, and to her discredit it must be said that in that she invariably succeeded. On the evening that Mr. Incoul crossed her vestibule, he was met by a hum of voices, broken by the rhythm of a waltz. The air was heavy, and in the hall was a smell of flowers and of food. The rooms were crowded. His friend Blydenburg was present and with him his daughter. The Wainwarings, whom he had always known, were also there, and there were other people by whom he had not been forgotten, and with whom he exchanged a word, but for Miss Barhyte he looked at first in vain.

He would have gone, a crowd was as irksome to him as solitude, but in passing an outer room elaborately supplied with paintings and bric-à-brac, he caught a glimpse of the girl talking with a young man whom he vaguely remembered to have seen in earlier days at his own home.

He walked in: Miss Barhyte greeted him as an old friend: there were other people near her, and the young man with whom she had been talking turned and joined them, and presently passed with them into another room.

Mr. Incoul found a seat beside the girl, and, after a little unimportant conversation asked her a question at which she started. But Mr. Incoul was not in haste for an answer, he told her that with her permission, he would do himself the honor of calling on her later, and, as the room was then invaded by some of her friends, he left her to them, and went his way.

CHAPTER II.
MISS BARHYTE AGREES TO CHANGE HER NAME.

A day or two after Mrs. Bachelor's reception, Mr. Incoul walked down Madison avenue, turned into one of the adjacent streets and rang the bell of a private boarding-house.

As he stood on the steps waiting for the door to be opened, a butcher-boy passed, whistling shrilly. Across the way a nurse-maid was idling with a perambulator, a slim-figured girl hurried by, a well-dressed woman descended from a carriage and a young man with a flower in his button-hole issued from a neighboring house. The nurse-maid stayed the perambulator and scrutinized the folds of the woman's gown; the young man eyed the hurrying girl; from the end of the street came the whistle of the retreating butcher, and as it fused into the rumble of Fifth avenue, Mr. Incoul heard the door opening behind him.

"Is Miss Barhyte at home?" he asked.

The servant, a negro, answered that she was.

"Then be good enough," said Mr. Incoul, "to take her this card."

The drawing-room, long and narrow, as is usual in many New York houses, was furnished in that fashion which is suggestive of a sheriff's sale, and best calculated to jar the nerves. Mr. Incoul did not wince. He gave the appointments one cursory, reluctant glance, and then went to the window. Across the way the nurse-maid still idled, the young man with a flower was drawing on a red glove, stitched with black, and as he looked out at them he heard a rustle, and turning, saw Miss Barhyte.

"I have come for an answer," he said simply.

"I am glad to see you," she answered, "very glad; I have thought much about what you said."

"Favorably, I hope."

"That must depend on you." She went to a bell and touched it. "Archibald," she said, when the negro appeared, "I am out. If any visitors come take them into the other room. Should any one want to come in here before I ring, say the parlor is being swept."

The man bowed and withdrew. He would have stood on his head for her. There were few servants that she did not affect in much the same manner. She seemed to win willingness naturally.

She seated herself on a sofa, and opposite to her Mr. Incoul found a chair. Her dress he noticed was of some dark material, tailor-made, and unrelieved save by a high white collar and the momentary glisten of a button. The cut and sobriety of her costume made her look like a handsome boy, a young Olympian as it were, one who had strayed from the games and been arrayed in modern guise. Indeed, her features suggested that combination of beauty and sensitiveness which was peculiar to the Greek lad, but her eyes were not dark—they were the blue victorious eyes of the Norseman—and her hair was red, the red of old gold, that red which partakes both of orange and of flame.

"I hope—" Mr. Incoul began, but she interrupted him.

"Wait," she said, "I have much to tell you of which the telling is difficult. Will you bear with me a moment?"

"Surely," he answered.

"It is this: It is needless for me to say I esteem you; it is unnecessary for me to say that I respect you, but it is because I do both that I feel I may speak frankly. My mother wishes me to marry you, but I do not. Let me tell you, first, that when my father died he left very little, but the little that he left seems to have disappeared, I do not know how or where. I know merely that we have next to nothing, and that we are in debt beside. Something, of course, has had to be done. I have found a position. Where do you suppose?" she asked, with a sudden smile and a complete change of key.

But Mr. Incoul had no surmises.

"In San Francisco! The MacDermotts, you know, the Bonanza people, want me to return with them and teach their daughter how to hold herself, and what not to say. It has been arranged that I am to go next week. Since the other night, however, my mother has told me to give up the MacDermotts and accept your offer. But that, of course, I cannot do."

"And why not?"

To this Miss Barhyte made no answer.

"You do not care for me, I know; there is slight reason why you should. Yet, might you not, perhaps, in time?"

The girl raised her eyebrows ever so slightly. "So you see," she continued, "I shall have to go to San Francisco."

Mr. Incoul remained silent a moment. "If," he said, at last, "if you will do me the honor to become my wife, in time you will care. It is painful for me to think of you accepting a position which at best is but a shade better than that of a servant, particularly so when I am able—nay, anxious," he added, pensively—"to surround you with everything which can make life pleasant. I am not old," he went on to say, "at least not so old that a marriage between us should seem incongruous. I find that I am sincerely attached to you— unselfishly, perhaps, would be the better word—and, if the privilege could be mine, the endeavor to make you happy would be to me more grateful than a second youth. Can you not accept me?"

He had been speaking less to her than to the hat which he held in his hand. The phrases had come from him haltingly, one by one, as though he had sought to weigh each mentally before dowering it with the wings of utterance, but, as he addressed this question he looked up at her. "Can you not?" he repeated.

Miss Barhyte raised a handkerchief to her lips and bit the shred of cambric with the *disinvoltura* of an heiress.

"Why is it," she queried, "why is it that marriage ever was invented? Why cannot a girl accept help from a man without becoming his wife?"

Mr. Incoul was about to reply that many do, but he felt that such a reply would be misplaced, and he called a platitude to his rescue. "There are wives and wives," he said.

"That is it," the girl returned, the color mounting to her cheeks; "if I could but be to you one of the latter."

He stared at her wonderingly, almost hopefully. "What do you mean?" he asked.

"Did you ever read 'Eugénie Grandet'?"

"No," he answered, "I never have."

"Well, I read it years ago. It is, I believe, the only one of Balzac's novels that young girls are supposed to read. It is tiresome indeed; I had almost forgotten it, but yesterday I remembered enough of the story to help me to come to some decision. In thinking the matter over and over again as I have done ever since I last saw you it has seemed that I could not become your wife unless you were willing to make the same agreement with me that Eugénie Grandet's husband made with her."

"What was the nature of that agreement?"

"It was that, though married, they were to live as though they were not married—as might brother and sister."

"Always?"

"Yes."

"No," Mr. Incoul answered, "to such an agreement I could not consent. Did I do so, I would be untrue to myself, unmanly to you. But if you will give me the right to aid you and yours, I will—according to my lights—leave nothing undone to make you contented; and if I succeed in so doing, if you are happy, then the agreement which you have suggested would fall of itself. Would it not?" he continued. "Would it not be baseless? See—" he added, and he made a vague gesture, but before he could finish the phrase, the girl's hands were before her face and he knew that she was weeping.

Mr. Incoul was not tender-hearted. He felt toward Miss Barhyte as were she some poem in flesh that it would be pleasant to make his own. In her carriage as in her looks, he had seen that stamp of breeding which is coercive even to the dissolute. In her eyes he had discerned that promise of delight which it is said the lost goddesses could convey; and at whose conveyance, the legend says, the minds of men were enraptured. It was in this wise that he felt to her. Such exhilaration as she may have brought him was of the spirit, and being cold by nature and undemonstrative, her tears annoyed him. He would have had her impassive, as befitted her beauty. Beside, he was annoyed at his own attitude. Why should there be sorrow where he had sought to bring smiles? But he had barely time to formulate his annoyance into a thing even as volatile as thought—the girl had risen and was leaving the room.

As she moved to the door Mr. Incoul hastened to open it for her, but she reached it before him and passed out unassisted.

When she had gone he noticed that the sun was setting and that the room was even more hideous than before. He went again to the window wondering how to act. The entire scene was a surprise to him. He had come knowing nothing of the girl's circumstances, and suddenly he learned that she was in indigence, unable perhaps to pay her board bills and worried by small tradesmen. He had come prepared to be refused and she had almost accepted him. But what an acceptance! In the nature of it his thoughts roamed curiously: he was to be a little more than kin, a little less than kind. She would accept him as a husband for out-of-door purposes, for the world's sake she would bear his name—at arm's length. According to the terms of her proposition were she ever really his wife it would be tantamount to a seduction. He was to be with her, and yet, until she so willed it, unable to call her his own. And did he refuse these terms, she was off, no one knew whither. But he had not refused, he told himself, he had indeed not refused, he had merely suggested an amendment which turned an impossibility into an allurement. What pleasanter thing could there be than the winning of one's own wife? The idea was so novel it delighted him. For the moment he preferred it to any other; beside it his former experience seemed humdrum indeed. But why had she wept? Her reasons, however, he had then no chance to elucidate. Miss Barhyte returned as abruptly as she had departed.

"Forgive me," she said, advancing to where he stood, "it was stupid of me to act as I did. I am sorry—are we still friends?" Her eyes were clear as had she never wept, but there were circles about them, and her face was colorless.

"Friends," he answered, "yes, and more—" He hesitated a moment, and then hastily added, "It is agreed, then, is it not, you will be my wife?"

"I will be your wife?"

"As Balzac's heroine was to her husband?"

"You have said it."

"But not always. If there come a time when you care for me, then I may ask you to give me your heart as to-day I have asked for your hand?"

"When that day comes, believe me," she said, and her delicious face took on a richer hue, "when that day comes there will be neither asking nor giving, we shall have come into our own."

With this assurance Mr. Incoul was fain to be content, and, after another word or two, he took his leave.

For some time after his departure, Miss Barhyte stood thinking. It had grown quite dark. Before the window a street lamp burned with a small, steady flame, but beyond, the azure of the electric light pervaded the adjacent square with a suggestion of absinthe and vice. One by one the opposite houses took on some form of interior illumination. A newsboy passed, hawking an extra with a noisy, aggressive ferocity as though he were angry with the neighborhood, and dared it come out and wrestle with him for his wares. There was a thin broken stream of shop-girls passing eastward; at intervals, men in evening dress sauntered leisurely to their dinners, to restaurants, or to clubland, and over the rough pavement there was a ceaseless rattle of traps and of wagons; the air was alive with the indefinable murmurs of a great city.

Miss Barhyte noticed none of these things. She had taken her former seat on the sofa and sat, her elbow on her crossed knee, her chin resting in her hand, while the fingers touched and barely separated her lips. The light from without was just strong enough to reach her feet and make visible the gold clock on her silk stocking, but her face was in the shadow as were her thoughts.

Presently she rose and rang the bell. "Archibald," she said, when the man came, and who at once busied himself with lighting the gas, "I want to send a note; can't you take it? It's only across the square."

"I'll have to be mighty spry about it, miss. The old lady do carry on most unreasonable if I go for anybody but herself. She has laws that strict they'd knock the Swedes and Prussians silly. Why, you wouldn't believe if I told you how—"

And Archibald ran on with an unbelievable tale of recent adventure with the landlady. But the girl feigned no interest. She had taken a card from her case. On it she wrote, *Viens ce soir*, and after running the pencil through her name, she wrote on the other side, Lenox Leigh, esq., Athenæum Club.

"There," she said, interrupting the negro in the very climax of his story, "it's for Mr. Leigh; you are sure to find him, so wait for an answer."

A fraction of an hour later, when Miss Barhyte took her seat at the dinner table, she found beside her plate a note that contained a single line: "Will be with you at nine. I kiss your lips. L. L."

CHAPTER III.
AFTER DARKNESS.

When Miss Barhyte was one year younger she had gone with her mother to pass the summer at Mt. Desert; and there, the morning of her arrival, on the monster angle of Rodick's porch, Lenox Leigh had caused himself to be presented.

A week later Miss Barhyte and her new acquaintance were as much gossiped about as was possible in that once unconventional resort.

Lenox Leigh was by birth a Baltimorean, and by profession a gentleman of leisure, yet as the exercise of that profession is considered less profitable in Baltimore than in New York, he had, for some time past, been domiciled in the latter city. From the onset he was well received; one of the Amsterdams had married a Leigh, his only sister had charmed the heart of Nicholas Manhattan, and being in this wise connected with two of the reigning families, he found the doors open as a matter of course. But even in the absence of potent relatives, there was no reason why he should not have been cordially welcomed. He was, it is true, better read than nineteen men out of twenty; when he went to the opera he preferred listening to the music to wandering from box to box; he declined to figure in cotillons and at no dinner, at no supper had he been known to drink anything stronger than claret and water.

But as an offset to these defects he was one of the most admirably disorganized young men that ever trod Fifth avenue. He was without beliefs and without prejudices; added to this he was indulgent to the failings of others, or perhaps it would be better to say that he was indifferent. It may be that the worst thing about him was that he was not bad enough; his wickedness, such as there was of it, was purely negative. A poet of the decadence of that period in fact when Rome had begun to weary of debauchery without yet acquiring a taste for virtue, a pre-mediæval Epicurean, let us say, could not have pushed a creedless refinement to a greater height than he. There were men who thought him a prig, and who said so when his back was turned.

It was in the company of this patrician of a later day that Miss Barhyte participated in the enjoyments of Mt. Desert. Leigh was then in his twenty-fifth year, and Miss Barhyte was just grazing the twenties. He was attractive in appearance, possessed of those features which now and then permit a man to do without beard or moustache, and his hair, which was black, clung so closely to his head that at a distance it might have been taken for the casque of a Saracen. To Miss Barhyte, as already noted, a full share of beauty had been allotted. Together they formed one of the most charming couples that it has ever been the historian's privilege to admire. And being a charming couple, and constantly together, they excited much interest in the minds of certain ladies who hailed from recondite Massachusettsian regions.

To this interest they were indifferent. At first, during the early evenings when the stars were put out by the Northern Lights, they rowed to the outermost shore of a neighboring island and lingered there for hours in an enchanted silence. Later, in the midsummer nights, when the harvest-moon was round and mellow, they wandered through the open fields back into the Dantesque forests and strayed in the clinging shadows and inviting solitudes of the pines.

From one such excursion they returned to the hotel at an hour which startled the night porter, who, in that capricious resort, should have lost his ability to be startled at anything.

That afternoon Mrs. Bunker Hill—one of the ladies to whom allusion has been made—approached Miss Barhyte on the porch. "And are you to be here much longer?" she asked, after a moment or two of desultory conversation.

"The holidays are almost over," the girl answered, with her radiant smile.

"*Holidays* do you call them? *Holidays* did I understand you to say? *I* should have called them *fast* days." And, with that elaborate witticism, Mrs. Bunker Hill shook out her skirts and sailed away.

Meanwhile an enveloping intimacy had sprung up between the two young people. Their conversation need not be chronicled. There was in it nothing unusual and nothing particularly brilliant; it was but a strain from that archaic duo in which we have all taken part and which at each repetition seems an original theme.

For the first time Miss Barhyte learned the intoxication of love. She gave her heart ungrudgingly, without calculation, without forethought, wholly, as a heart should be given and freely as had the gift been consecrated in the nave of a cathedral. If she were generous why should she be blamed? In the giving she found that mite of happiness, that one unclouded day that is fair as June roses and dawns but once.

In September Miss Barhyte went with her mother on a visit in the Berkshire Hills. Leigh journeyed South. A matter of business claimed his attention in Baltimore, and when, early in November, he reached New York the girl had already returned.

Since the death of Barhyte *père* she had lived with her mother in a small house in Irving Place, which they rented, furnished, by the year. But on this particular autumn affairs had gone so badly, some stock had depreciated, some railroad had been mismanaged, or some trustee had speculated—something, in fact, had happened of which no one save those personally interested ever know or ever care, and, as a result, the house in Irving Place was given up, and the mother and daughter moved into a boarding-house.

Of all this Lenox Leigh was made duly aware. Had he been able, and could such a thing have been proper and conventional, he would have been glad indeed to offer assistance; he was not selfish, but then he was not rich, a condition which always makes unselfishness easy. Matrimony was out of the question; his income was large enough to permit him to live without running into debt, but beyond that its flexibility did not extend, and in money matters, and in money matters alone, Lenox Leigh was the most scrupulous of men. Beside, as the phrase goes, he was not a marrying man—marriage, he was accustomed to assert, means one woman more and one man less, and beyond that definition he steadfastly declined to look, except to announce that, like some other institutions, matrimony was going out of fashion.

That winter Miss Barhyte was more circumspect. It was not that her affection had faltered, but in the monochromes of a great city the primal glamour that was born of the fields and of the sea lost its lustre. Then, too, Lenox in the correctness of evening dress was not the same adorer who had lounged in flannels at her side, and the change from the open country to the boarding-house parlor affected their spirits unconsciously.

And so the months wore away. There were dinners and routs which the young people attended in common, there were long walks on avenues unfrequented by fashion, and there were evenings prearranged which they passed together and during which the girl's mother sat up stairs and thought her own thoughts.

Mrs. Barhyte had been a pretty woman and inconsequential, as pretty woman are apt to be. Her girlhood had been of the happiest, without a noteworthy grief. She married one whose perfection had seemed to her impeccable, and then suddenly without a monition the tide of disaster set in. After the birth of a second child, Maida, her husband began to drink, and drank, after each debauch with a face paler than before, until disgrace came and with it a plunge into the North River. Her elder child, a son, on whom she placed her remaining hopes, had barely skirted manhood before he was taken from her to die of small-pox in a hospital. Then came a depreciation in the securities which she held and in its train the small miseries of the shabby genteel. Finally, the few annual thousands that were left to her seemed to evaporate, and as she sat in her room alone her thoughts were bitter. The pretty inconsequential girl had developed into a woman, hardened yet unresigned.

At forty-five her hair was white, her face was colorless as her widow's cap, her heart was dead.

On the night when her daughter, under the chaperonage of Mrs. Hildred, one of her few surviving relatives—returned from the reception, she was still sitting up. At Mrs. Hildred's suggestion a position, to which allusion has been made, had been offered to her daughter, and that position—the bringing up or rather the bringing out of a child of the West—she determined that her daughter should accept. Afterwards—well, perhaps for Maida there were other things in store, as for herself she expected little. She would betake herself to some Connecticut village and there wait for death.

When her daughter entered the room she was sitting in the erect impassibility of a statue. Her eyes indeed were restless, but her face was dumb, and in the presence of that silent desolation, the girl's tender heart was touched.

"Mother!" she exclaimed, "why did you wait up for me?" And she found a seat on the sofa near her mother and took her hand caressingly in her own. "Why are you up so late," she continued, "are you not tired? Oh, mother," the girl cried, impetuously, "if you only knew what happened to-night—what do you suppose?"

But Mrs. Barhyte shook her head, she had no thoughts left for suppositions. And quickly, for the mere sake of telling something that would arouse her mother if ever so little from her apathy, Maida related Mr. Incoul's offer. Her success was greater, if other, than she anticipated. It was as though she had poured into a parching throat the very waters of life. It was the post tenebras, lux. And what a light! The incandescence of unexpected hope. A cataract of gold pieces could not have been more dazzling; it was blinding after the shadows in which she had groped. The color came to her cheeks, her hand grew moist. "Yes, yes," she cried, urging the girl's narrative with a motion of the head like to that of a jockey speeding to the post; "yes, yes," she repeated, and her restless eyes flamed with the heat of fever.

"Wasn't it odd?" Maida concluded abruptly.

"But you accepted him?" the mother asked hoarsely, almost fiercely.

"Accepted him? No, of course not—he—why, mother, what is the matter?"

Engrossed in the telling of her story, the girl had not noticed her mother's agitation, but at her last words, at the answer to the question, her wrist had been caught as in a vise, and eyes that she no longer recognized—eyes dilated with anger, desperation and revulsion of feeling—were staring into her own. Instinctively she drew back—"Oh, mother, what is it?" And the mother bending forward, even as the daughter retreated, hissed, "You shall accept him—I say you shall!"

"Mother, mother," the girl moaned, helplessly.

"You shall accept him, do you hear me?"

"But, mother, how can I?" The tears were rolling down her cheeks, she was frightened—the acute, agonizing fright of a child pursued. She tried to free herself, but the hands on her wrist only tightened, and her mother's face, livid now, was close to her own.

"You shall accept him," she repeated with the insistence of a monomaniac. And the girl, with bended head, through the paroxysms of her sobs, could only murmur in piteous, beseeching tones, "Mother! mother!"

But to the plaint the woman was as deaf as her heart was dumb. She indeed loosened her hold and the girl fell back on the lounge from which they had both arisen, but it was only to summon from the reservoirs of her being some new strength wherewith to vanquish. For a moment she stood motionless, watching the girl quiver in her emotion, and as the sobbing subsided, she stretched forth her hand again, and caught her by the shoulder.

"Look up at me," she said, and the girl, obedient, rose from her seat and gazed imploringly in her mother's face. No Neapolitan fish-wife was ever more eager to barter her daughter than was this lady of acknowledged piety and refinement, and the face into which her daughter looked and shrank from bore no trace of pity or compassion. "Tell me if you dare," she continued, "tell me why it is that you refuse? What more do you want? Are you a princess of the blood? Perhaps you will say you don't love him! And what if you don't? I loved your father and look at me now! Beside, you have had enough of that—there, don't stare at me in that way. I know, and so do you. Now take your choice—accept this offer or get to your lover—and this very night. As for me, I disown you, I—"

But the flood of words was interrupted—the girl had fainted. The simulachre of death had extended its kindly arms, and into them she had fallen as into a grateful release.

By the morrow her spirit was broken. Two days later Mr. Incoul called with what success the reader has been already informed, and on that same evening in obedience to the note, came Lenox Leigh.

CHAPTER IV.
AN EVENING CALL.

When Leigh entered the drawing-room he found Miss Barhyte already there. "It is good of you to come," she said, by way of greeting.

The young man advanced to where she stood, and in a tender, proprietary manner, took her hand in his; he would have kissed her, but she turned her face aside.

"What is it?" he asked; "you are pale as Ophelia."

"And you, my prince, as inquisitive as Hamlet."

She led him to a seat and found one for herself. Her eyes rested in his own, and for a moment both were silent.

"Lenox," she asked at last, "do you know Mr. Incoul?"

"Yes, of course; every one does."

"I mean do you know him well?"

"I never said ten words to him, nor he to me."

"So much the better. What do you suppose he did the other evening after you went away?"

"Really, I have no idea, but if you wish me to draw on my imagination, I suppose he went away too."

"He offered himself."

"For what?"

"To me."

"Maida, that mummy! You are joking."

"No, I am not joking, nor was he."

"Well, what then?"

"Then, as you say, he went away."

"And what did you do?"

"I went away too."

"Be serious; tell me about it."

"He came here this afternoon, and I—well—I am to be Mrs. Incoul."

Lenox bit his lip. Into his face there came an expression of angered resentment. He stood up from his seat; the girl put out her hand as though to stay him: "Lenox, I had to," she cried. But he paid no attention to her words and crossed the room.

On the mantel before him was a clock that ticked with a low, dolent moan, and for some time he stood looking at it as were it an object of peculiar interest which he had never before enjoyed the leisure to examine. But the clock might have swooned from internal pain, he neither saw nor heard it; his thoughts circled through episodes of the winter back to the forest and the fringes of the summer sea. And slowly the anger gave way to wonder, and presently the wonder faded and in its place there came a sentiment like that of sorrow, a doubled sorrow in whose component parts there was both pity and distress.

It is said that the rich are without appreciation of their wealth until it is lost or endangered, and it was not until that evening that Lenox Leigh appreciated at its worth the loveliness that was slipping from him. He knew then that he might tread the highroads and faubourgs of two worlds with the insistence of the Wandering Jew, and yet find no one so delicious as she. And in the first flood of his anger he felt as were he being robbed, as though the one thing that had lifted him out of the brutal commonplaces of the every day was being caught up and carried beyond the limits of vision. And into this resentment there came the suspicion that he was not alone being robbed, that he was being cheated to boot, that the love which he had thought to receive as he had seemed to give love before, was an illusory representation, a phantom constructed of phrases.

But this suspicion faded; he knew untold that the girl's whole heart was his, had been his, was yet his and probably would be his for all of time, till the grave opened and closed again. And then the wonder came. He knew, none better, the purity of her heart, and knowing, too, her gentleness, the sweetness of her nature, her abnegation of self, he began to understand that some tragedy had been enacted which he had not been called upon to witness. Of her circumstances he had been necessarily informed. But in the sensitiveness of her refinement the girl had shrunk from unveiling to a lover's eyes the increasing miseries of her position, and of the poignancy of those miseries he had now, uninformed, an inkling. If she sold herself, surely it was because the sale was imperative. The white impassible face of the girl's mother rose before him and then, at once, he understood her cry, "Lenox, I had to."

As he moved from her, Maida had seen the anger, and knowing the anger to be as just as justice ever is, she shook her head in helpless grief, yet her eyes were tearless as had she no tears left to shed. She had seen the anger, but ignorant of the phases of thought by which it had been transfigured she stole up to where he stood and touched his arm with a shrinking caress.

He turned and would have caught her to him, but she drew back, elusively, as might a swan. "No, not that, Lenox. Only say that you do not hate me. Lenox, if you only knew. To me it is bitterer than death. You are the whole world to me, yet never must I see you again. If I could but tell you all. If I could but tell him all, if there were anything that I could do or say, but there is nothing, nothing," she added pensively, "except submission."

Her voice had sunk into a whisper: she was pleading as much with herself as with him. Her arms were pendant and her eyes downcast. On the mantel the clock kept up its low, dolorous moan, as though in sympathy with her woe. "Nothing," she repeated.

"But surely it need not be. Things cannot be so bad as that—Maida, I cannot lose you. If nothing else can be done, let us go away; at its best New York is tiresome; we could both leave it without a regret or a wish to return. And then, there is Italy; we have but to choose. Why, I could take a palace on the Grand Canal for less than I pay for my rooms at the Cumberland. And you would love Venice; and in winter there is Capri and Sorrento and Palermo. I have known days in Palermo when I seemed to be living in a haze of turquoise and gold. And the nights! You should see the nights! The stars are large as lilies! See, it would be so easy; in a fortnight we could be in Genoa, and before we got there we would have been forgotten."

He was bending forward speaking rapidly, persuasively, half hoping, half fearing, she would accept. She did not interrupt him, and he continued impetuously, as though intoxicated on his own words.

"When we are tired of the South, there are the lakes and that lovely Tyrol; there will be so much to do, so much to see. After New York, we shall really seem to live; and then, beyond, is Munich—you are sure to love that city." He hated Munich; he hated Germany. The entire land, and everything that was in it, was odious to him; but for the moment he forgot. He would have said more, even to praises of Berlin, but the girl raised her ringless hand and shook her head wearily.

"No, Lenox, it may not be. Did I go with you, in a year—six months, perhaps—we would both regret. It would be not only expatriation; it would, for me at least, be isolation as well, and, though I would bear willingly with both, you would not. You think so now, perhaps, I do not doubt"—and a phantom of a smile crossed her face—"and I thank you for so thinking, but it may not be."

Her hand fell to her side, and she turned listlessly away. "You must forget me, Lenox—but not too soon, will you?"

"Never, sweetheart—never!"

"Ah, but you must. And I must learn to forget you. It will be difficult. No one can be to me what you have been. You have been my youth, Lenox; my girlhood has been yours. I have nothing left. Nothing except regrets—regrets that youth should pass so quickly and that girlhood comes but once."

Her lips were tremulous, but she was trying to be brave.

"But surely, Maida, it cannot be that we are to part forever. Afterwards—" the word was vague, but they both understood—"afterwards I may see you. Such things often are. Because you feel yourself compelled to this step, there is no reason why I, of all others, should be shut out of your life."

"It is the fact of your being the one of all others that makes the shutting needful."

"It shall not be."

"Lenox," she pleaded, "it is harder for me than for you."

"But how can you ask me, how can you think that I will give you up? The affair is wretched enough as it is, and now, by insisting that I am not to see you again, you would make it even worse. People think it easy to love, but it is not; I know nothing more difficult. You are the only one for whom I have ever cared. It was not difficult to do so, I admit, but the fact remains. I have loved you, I have loved you more and more every day, and now, when I love you most, when I love you as I can never love again, you find it the easiest matter in the world to come to me and say, 'It's ended; *bon jour.*'"

"You are cruel, Lenox, you are cruel."

"It is you that are cruel, and there the wonder is, for your cruelty is unconscious, of your own free will you would not know how."

"It is not that I am cruel, it is that I am trying to do right. And it is for you to aid me. I have been true to you, do not ask me now to be false to myself."

If at that moment Mrs. Bunker Hill could have looked into the girl's face, her suspicions would have vanished into air. Maida needed only a less fashionable gown to look like a mediæval saint; and before the honesty that was in her eyes Lenox bowed his head.

"Will you help me?"

"I will," he answered.

"I knew you would; you are too good to try to make me more miserable than I am. And now, you must go; kiss me, it is the last time."

He caught her in his arms and kissed her full upon the mouth. He kissed her wet eyes, her cheeks, the splendor of her hair. And after a moment of the acutest pain of all her life, the girl freed herself from his embrace, and let him go without another word.

CHAPTER V.
A YELLOW ENVELOPE.

There is a peculiarity about Baden-Baden which no other watering-place seems to share—it has the aroma of a pretty woman. In August it is warm, crowded, enervating, tiresome as are all warm and crowded places, but the air is delicately freighted and a pervasive fragrance is discerned even by the indifferent.

In the summer that succeeded Maida's marriage Baden was the same tame, perfumed *zwei und funfzig* that it has ever been since the war. The ladies and gentlemen who were to regard it as a sort of continuation of the Bois de Boulogne had departed never to return. Gone was Benazet, gone, too, the click of the roulette ball. The echoes and uproars of the Second Empire had died away, as echoes and uproars ever must, and in place of the paint and cleverness of the *dames du-lac* had come the stupid loveliness of the *schwärmerisch Mädchen*.

But though Paris had turned her wicked back, the attitude of that decadent capital in no wise affected other cities. On the particular August to which allusion is made, interminable dinners were consumed by contingents from the politest lands, and also from some that were semi-barbaric.

In the Lichenthal Allée and on the promenade in front of the Kursaal one could hear six languages in as many minutes, and given a polyglottic ear the number could have been increased to ten. Among those who added their little quota to this summer Babel were Mr. and Mrs. Incoul.

The wedding had been very simple. Mrs. Barhyte had wished the ceremony performed in Grace Church, and to the ceremony she had also wished that all New York should be bidden. To her it represented a glory which in the absence of envious witnesses would be lustreless indeed. But in this respect her wishes were disregarded. On a melting morning in early June, a handful of people, thirty at most, assembled in Mrs. Hildred's drawing-room. The grave service that is in usage among Episcopalians was mumbled by a diligent bishop, there was a hurried and heavy breakfast, and two hours later the bride and groom were on the deck of the "Umbria."

The entire affair had been conducted with the utmost dispatch. The *Sunday Sun* chronicled the engagement in one issue, and gave the date of the wedding in the next. It was not so much that Harmon Incoul was ardent in his wooing or that Miss Barhyte was anxious to assume the rank and privileges that belong to the wedded state. The incentives were other if equally prosaic. The ceremony if undergone needed to be undergone at once. Summer was almost upon them, and in the code which society has made for itself, summer weddings are reproved. There was indeed some question of postponing the rites until autumn. But on that Mrs. Barhyte put her foot. She was far from sure of her daughter, and as for the other contracting party, who could tell but that he might change his mind. Such changes had been, and instances of such misconduct presented themselves unsummoned to the woman's mind. The fish had been landed almost without effort, a fish more desirable than any other, a very prize among fishes, and the possibility that he might slip away and without so much as a gill awry float off into clearer and less troubled seas, nerved her to her task anew.

In the interview which she enjoyed with her prospective son-in-law she was careful, however, to display no eagerness. She was sedate when sedateness seemed necessary, but her usual attitude was one of conciliatory disinterestedness. Her daughter's choice she told him had met with her fullest approval, and it was to her a matter of deep regret that neither her husband nor her father—the late Chief Justice Hildred, with whose name Mr. Incoul was of course familiar—that neither of them had been spared to join in the expression of her satisfaction. Of Maida it was unnecessary to speak, yet this at least should be said, she was young and she was impressionable, as young people are apt to be, but she had never given her mother cause for the slightest vexation, not the slightest. "She is a sweet girl," Mrs. Barhyte went on to say, "and one with an admirable disposition; she takes after her father in that, but she has her grandfather's intellect."

"Her beauty, madam, comes from you."

To this Mrs. Barhyte assented. "She is pretty," she said, and then in the voice of an actress who feels her rôle, "Do be good to her," she pleaded, "she is all I have."

Mr. Incoul assured her that on that score she need give herself no uneasiness, and a few days before the wedding, begged as a particular favor to himself that after the ceremony she would take up her residence in his house. The servants, he explained, had been instructed in that respect, and a checkbook of the Chemical Bank would be handed her in defrayment of all expenses. "And to think," Mrs. Barhyte muttered to herself, "to think that I might have died in Connecticut!"

The voyage over was precisely like any other. There were six days of discomfort in the open, and between Queenstown and Liverpool unnumbered hours of gloomy and irritating delay. Mrs. Incoul grew weary of the captain's cabin and her husband was not enthusiastic on the subject of the quarters which the first officer had relinquished to him. But in dear old

London, as all good Americans are wont to call that delightful city, Mrs. Incoul's spirits revived. The difference between Claridge's and Rodick's would have interested one far more apathetic than she, and as she had never before set her foot on Piccadilly, and as Rotten Row and Regent Circus were as unfamiliar to her as the banks of the Yang-tse-Kiang, she had none of that satiated feeling of the *déjà-vu* which besets the majority of us on our travels.

The notice of their arrival in the *Morning Post* had been followed by cards without limit and invitations without stint. An evening gazette published an editorial a column in length, in which after an historical review of wealth from Plutus to the Duke of Westminster, the reader learned that the world had probably never seen a man so rich and yet seemingly so unconscious of the power which riches give as was Harmon Incoul, esq., of New York, U. S. A.

During the few weeks that were passed in London the bride and groom were bidden to more crushes, dinners and garden parties than Maida had attended during the entire course of her bud-hood. There was the inevitable presentation and as the girl's face was noticeably fair she and her husband were made welcome at Marlborough House. Afterwards, yet before the season drooped, there was a trip to Paris, a city, which, after the splendors of London, seemed cheap and tawdry indeed, and then as already noted came the villegiatura at Babel-Baden.

Meanwhile Maida had come and gone, eaten and fasted, danced and driven in a constant chase after excitement. To her husband she had acted as she might have done to some middle-aged cousin with whom she was not precisely on that which is termed a familiar footing, one on whom chance not choice had made her dependent, and to whom in consequence much consideration was due. But her relations will be perhaps better understood when it is related that she had not found herself physically capable of calling him by his given name, or in fact anything else than You. It was not that she disliked him, on the contrary, in many ways he was highly sympathetic, but the well-springs of her affection had been dried, and the season of their refreshment was yet obscure.

In the face of this half-hearted platonism Mr. Incoul had displayed a wisdom which was peculiar to himself; he exacted none of those little tributes which are conceded to be a husband's due, and he allowed himself none of the familiarities which are reported to be an appanage of the married state. From the beginning he had determined to win his wife by the exercise of that force which, given time and opportunity, a strong nature invariably exerts over a weaker one. He was indulgent but he was also austere. The ordering of one gown or of five hundred was a matter of which he left her sole mistress. Had she so desired she might have bought a jewelry shop one day and given it back as a free gift on the morrow. But on a question of ethics he allowed no appeal. The Countess of Ex, a lady of dishonor at a popular court, had, during the London season, issued cards for a ball. On the evening on which it was to take place the bride and groom had dined at one house, and gone to a musicale at another. When leaving the latter entertainment Maida told her husband to tell the man "Park Lane." Mr. Incoul, however, ordered the carriage to be driven to the hotel.

"Did you not understand me?" she asked. "I am going to the Countess of Ex's."

"She is not a woman whom I care to have you know," he replied.

"But the Prince is to be there!"

To this he assented. "Perhaps." And then he added in a voice that admitted of no further argument, "But not my wife."

Maida sank back in the carriage startled by an unexperienced emotion. For the first time since the wedding she could have kissed the man whose name she bore. It was in this way that matters shaped themselves.

Soon after reaching Paris, Mr. Blydenburg called. He had brought his daughter abroad because he did not know what else to do with her, and now that he was on the Continent he did not know what to do with himself. He explained these pre-occupations and Mr. Incoul suggested that in the general exodus they should all go to Germany. To this suggestion Blydenburg gave a ready assent and that very day purchased a translation of Tacitus, a copy of Mr. Baring-Gould's Germany, a Baedeker, and a remote edition of Murray.

At the appointed date the little party started for Cologne, where, after viewing a bone of the fabulous virgin Undecemilla, they drifted to Frankfort and from there reached the Oos. In Baden, Blydenburg and his daughter elected domicile at the Englischerhof, while through the foresight of a courier, good-looking, polyglottic, idle and useful, the Incouls found a spacious apartment in the Villa Wilhelmina, a belonging of the Mesmer House.

In the drawer of the table which Maida selected as a suitable place for superfluous rings was a yellow envelope addressed to the Gräfin von Adelsburg. On the back was an attempt at addition, a double column of figures which evidently represented the hotel expenses of the lady to whom the envelope was addressed. The figures were marked carefully that no mistake should be possible, but the sum total had been jotted down in hurried numerals, as though the mathematician had been irritated at the amount, while under all, in an indignant scrawl, was the legend "S. T."

Maida was the least inquisitive of mortals, but one evening, a week or ten days after her arrival, when she happened to be sitting in company with the

Blydenburgs and her husband on the broad terrace that fronts the Kursaal, she alluded, for the mere sake of conversation, to the envelope which she had found. The Gräfin von Adelsburg it then appeared was the name with which the Empress of a neighboring realm was accustomed to veil her rank, and the legend it was suggested could only stand for *schrechlich theuer*, frightfully dear. The Empress had vacated the Villa Wilhelmina but a short time before and it seemed not improbable that the figures and conclusion were in her own imperial hand.

While this subject was under discussion the Prince of Albion sauntered down the walk. He was a handsome man, with blue projecting eyes, somewhat stout, perhaps, but not obese. In his train were two ladies and a few men. As he was about to pass Mrs. Incoul he stopped and raised his hat. It was of soft felt, she noticed, and his coat was tailless. He uttered a few amiable commonplaces and then moved on. The terrace had become very crowded. The little party had found seats near the musicians, and from either side came a hum of voices. A Saxon halted before them, designating with pointing finger the retreating back of the Prince, his companion, a pinguid woman who looked as though she lived on fish, shouted, "*Herr Jesus! ist es ja möglich*," and hurried on for a closer view. Near by was a group of Brazilians and among them a pretty girl in a fantastic gown, whose voice was like the murmur of birds. To the left were some Russians conversing in a hard, cruel French. The girl seemed to have interested them. "But why," asked one, "but why is it that she wears such loud colors?" To which another, presumably the wit of the party, answered idly, "Who knows, she may be deaf." And immediately behind Mrs. Incoul were two young Americans, wonderfully well dressed, who were exchanging chaste anecdotes and recalling recent adventures with an accompaniment of smothered laughter that was fathomless in its good-fellowship.

Maida paid no attention to the conversation about her. She was thinking of the yellow envelope, and for the first time she began to form some conception of her husband's wealth. Apparently he thought nothing of prices that seemed exorbitant to one whose coffers notoriously overflowed. She had never spoken to him about money, nor he to her; she knew merely that his purse was open; yet, as is usual with one who has been obliged to count the pennies, she had in her recent shopping often hesitated and refused to buy. In Paris she had chaffered over handkerchiefs and been alarmed at Doucet's bill. Indeed at Virot's when she told that poetic milliner what she wished to pay for a bonnet, Virot, smiling almost with condescension, had said to her, "The *chapeau* that madame wants is surely a *chapeau en Espagne*."

And now for the first time she began to understand. She saw how much was hers, how ungrudgingly it was given, how easy her path was made, how pleasant it might be for the rest of her days, and she half-turned and looked at her husband. If she could only forget, she thought, only forget and begin anew. If she could but tell him all! She moaned to herself. The moon was shining behind the Kursaal and in the air was the usual caress. The musicians, who had just attacked and subdued the Meistersänger, began a sob of Weber's that had been strangled into a waltz, and as the measures flowed they brought her that pacification which music alone can bring.

The past was over and done, ill-done, she knew, but above it might grow such weeds of forgetfulness as would hide it even from herself. In a semi-unconsciousness of her surroundings she stared like a pretty sphinx into the future. The waltz swooned in its ultimate accords, but she had ceased to hear; it had lulled and left her; her thoughts roamed far off into distant possibilities; she was dreaming with eyes wide open.

Abruptly the orchestra attacked a score that was seasoned with red pepper—the can-can of an opéra-bouffe: the notes exploded like fire crackers, and in the explosion brought vistas of silk stockings, whirlwinds of disordered skirts, the heat and frenzy of an orgy. And then, as the riot mounted like a flame, suddenly in a clash and shudder of brass the uproar ceased.

Maida, aroused from her revery by the indecency of the music, looked idly about her. The Russians were drinking beer that was as saffron as their own faces. The Brazilians had departed. The young Americans were smoking Bond street cigarettes which they believed to be Egyptian, and discussing the relative merits of Hills and Poole.

"While I was getting measured for that top coat you liked so much," said one, "Leigh came in."

"Lee? What Lee? Sumpter?"

"No; Lenox Leigh."

"Did he, though? How was he?"

"Finest form. Said he would take in Paris and Baden. He may be here now for all I know. Let's ask the waiter for a Fremden-List."

Maida had heard, and with the hearing there had come to her an enveloping dread. She felt that, did she see him, the love which she had tried to banish would return unfettered from its exile. Strength was not yet hers; with time, she knew, she could have sworn it would come; but, for the moment, she was helpless, and into the dread a longing mingled. At once, as though in search of a protection that should guard her against herself, she turned to her husband. To him, the Russians, Brazilians, and other gentry had been part of the landscape. He had little taste for music, and Blydenburg had bored him as that amiable gentleman was accustomed to bore every one with whom he conversed, yet, nevertheless, through that spirit of paradox which is common to us all, Mr. Incoul liked the man, and for old association's sake took to the boredom in a kindlier fashion than had it come from a newer and more vivacious acquaintance. Blydenburg had been explaining the value of recent excavations in Tirynth, a subject which Mr. Incoul understood better than the informist, but he noticed Maida's movement and stopped short.

"Come, Milly," he said to his daughter, "let's be going."

Milly had sat by his side the entire evening, in stealthy enjoyment of secular music, performed for the first time in her hearing on the Lord's day. She was a pale, freckled girl, with hair of the shade of Bavarian beer. She was not beautiful, but then she was good—a sort of angel bound in calf.

When Milly and her father had disappeared, Maida turned to her husband again. "Do you mind leaving Baden?" she asked.

Mr. Incoul eyed her a moment. "Why?" he asked. He had a trick of answering one question with another, yet for the moment she wondered whether he too had heard the conversation behind them, and then comforted by the thought that in any case the name of Lenox Leigh could convey but little to him, she shrugged her shoulders. "Oh, I don't know," she said; "I don't like it; it's hot and crowded. I think I would like the seashore better."

"Very good," he answered; "whatever you prefer. I will speak to Karl to-night." (Karl was the courier.) "I don't suppose," he added, reflectively, "that you would care for Trouville—I know I should not."

He had risen, and Maida, who had risen with him, was looking down at the gravel, which she toyed nervously with her foot. The opera that had been given that evening was evidently over. A stream of people were coming from the direction of the theatre, and among them was the Prince. He was chatting with his companions, but his trained eye had marked Mrs. Incoul, and when he reached the place where she stood he stopped again.

"You didn't go in to-night," he said, collectively. "It was rather good, too." And then, without waiting for an answer, he continued: "Won't you both dine with us to-morrow?"

"Oh, we can't," Maida answered. She was tormented with the thought that at any moment Lenox might appear. "We can't; we are going away."

The Prince smiled in his brown beard. Americans were popular with him. He liked their freedom. There was, he knew, barely one woman in Baden, not utterly bedridden, who would have taken his invitation so lightly. "I am sorry," he said, and he spoke sincerely. Like any other sensible man, he liked beauty and he liked it near him. He knew that Mrs. Incoul had been recently married, and in his own sagacious way, *il posait des jalons*. "You are to be at Ballaster in the autumn, I hear." Ballaster was a commodious shooting-box in Scotland, the possession of an hospitable peer.

"Yes, I believe we are," Maida answered.

"I hope to see you there," and with these historic words, Prince Charming departed.

CHAPTER VI.
BIARRITZ

After a frühstück of coffee and honey, to which the inn-keeper, out of compliment to the nationality of his guest, had added an ear of green corn— a combination, be it said, that no one but a German could have imagined— Mr. Incoul went in search of his friend.

He had questioned Karl, and the courier had spoken of Ostend with such enthusiasm that his employer suspected him of some personal interest in the place and struck it at once from the list of possible resorts which he had been devising. On the subject of other *bains de mer* the man was less communicative. There was, he said, nothing attractive about Travemunde, except the name; Scheveningen was apt to be chilly; Trouville he rather favored, but to his thinking Ostend was preferable.

When the courier had gone Mr. Incoul ran his eye down a mental map of the coast of France, and just as it reached the Spanish frontier he remembered that some one in his hearing had recently sounded the attractions of Biarritz. On that seaboard he ultimately decided, and it was with the idea that Blydenburg might go further and fare worse that he sought his friend and suggested the advantages of a trip to the Basque country.

Mr. Blydenburg had few objections to make. He had taken very kindly to the consumption of beer, but beer had not agreed with him, and he admitted, did he stay in Baden, that, in spite of the ill effects, he would still be unable to resist the allurements of that insidious beverage. "Act like a man, then," said Mr. Incoul, encouragingly; "act like a man and flee from it."

There was no gainsaying the value of this advice, but between its adoption and a journey to Biarritz the margin was wide. "It is true," he said, reflectively, "I could study the language at the fountain-head." (Mr. Blydenburg, it may be explained, was a gentleman who plumed himself on his familiarity with recondite tongues, but one whose knowledge of the languages that are current in polite society was such as is gleaned from the appendices of guide-books.)

Mr. Incoul nodded approvingly, "Certainly there would be no difficulty about that."

Blydenburg looked at him musingly for a moment and nodded, too. "The name Biarritz," he said, "comes, I am inclined to believe, from bi haritz— two oaks. Minucius thinks that it comes from bi harri—two rocks; but I have detected Minucius in certain errors which has made me wary of accepting his opinion. For instance, he claims that the Basques are descendants of the Phœnicians. Nothing could be more preposterous. They are purely Iberian, and probably the most ancient race in Europe. Why, you would be surprised"—

Mr. Incoul interrupted him cruelly—"I often am," he said; "now tell me, will you be ready this afternoon?"

"The laundress has just taken my things."

"Send after them, then. I make no doubt that there you can find another on the Bay of Biscay."

"I wonder what Biscay comes from? bi scai, two currents, perhaps. Yes, of course, I will be ready." And as his friend moved away, he pursed his lips abstractedly and made a note of the derivation.

A courier aiding, the journey from Baden to Biarritz can be accomplished without loss of life or reason. It partakes something of the character of a zigzag, the connections are seldom convenient, the wayside inns are not of the best, but if people go abroad to be uncomfortable, what more can the heart desire? The Incoul-Blydenburg party, impeded by Karl, a body-servant, and two maids, received their allotted share of discomfort with the very best grace in the world. They reached Bayonne after five days, not, it is true, of consecutive motion, but of such consecutive heat that they were glad to descend at the station of that excitable little city and in the fresh night air drive in open carriages over the few kilometres that remained to be traversed.

It was many hours before the journey was sufficiently a part of the past to enable the travelers to look about them, but on the evening succeeding their arrival, after a dinner on the verandah of the Continental, they sat with much contentment of spirit enjoying the intermittent showers of summer stars and the boom and rustle of the waves. Baden was unregretted. To the left, high above, on the summit of a projecting eminence, the white and illuminated Casino glittered like an ærian palace. To the right was the gardened quadrangle of the former Empress of the French, in the air was the scent of seaweed and before them the Infinite.

"It's quite good enough for me," Blydenburg confided to his companions, and the confidence in its inelegant terseness conveyed the sentiments of them all.

A week passed without bringing with it any incident worthy of record. In the mornings they met at the Moorish Pavilion which stands on the shore and there lounged or bathed. Maida's beauty necessarily attracted much attention, and when she issued in a floating wrapper from the sedan-chair in which she allowed herself to be carried from the Pavilion to the sea, a number of amateurs who stood each day just out of reach of the waves, expressed their admiration in winning gutturals.

She was, assuredly, very beautiful, particularly so in comparison with the powdered sallowness of the ladies from Spain, and when, with a breezy gesture of her own, she tossed her wrap to the bather and with sandaled feet and a white and clinging costume of serge she stepped to the water there was one on-looker who bethought him of a nymph of the Ægean Sea. She was a good swimmer, as the American girl often is, and she breasted and dived through the wonderful waves with an intrepidity such as the accompanying *baigneur* had been rarely called upon to restrain.

From the shade of beach chairs, large and covered like wicker tents, her husband and the Blydenburgs would watch her prowess, and when, after a final ride on the crest of some great billow, she would be tossed breathless and deliciously disheveled into the steadying arms of the bather, the amateurs were almost tempted to applaud.

In the afternoons there were drives and excursions. One day to Bayonne along the white, hard road that skirts the Chambre d'Amour, through the peace and quiet of Aiglet and on through kilometres of pines to the Adour, a river so beautiful in itself that all the ingenuity of man has been unable to make it wholly hideous, and thence by its banks to the outlying gardens of the city.

On other days they would loiter on the cliffs that overhang the Côte des Basques, or push on to Bidart, a chromatic village where the inhabitants are so silent that one might fancy them enchanted by the mellow marvels of their afternoons.

But of all other places Maida preferred Saint Jean-de-Luz. It lies near the frontier on a bay of the tenderest blue, and for background it has the hazy amethyst of the neighborly Pyrenees. The houses are rainbows of blended colors; from the open door-ways the passer, now and then, catches a whiff of rancid oil, the smell of victuals cooked in fat, from a mouldering square a cathedral casts an unexpected chill, but otherwise the town is charming, warm and very bright. On the shore stands an inn and next to it a toy casino.

To this exotic resort the little party drove one afternoon. It had been originally arranged to pass the day there, but on the day for which the excursion was planned, a *Course Landaise* was announced at Biarritz, and it was then decided that they should first view the *course* and dine afterwards at Saint Jean. At first both Maida and Miss Blydenburg refused to attend the performance and it was not until they were assured that it was a bull-fight for ladies in which there was no shedding of blood that they consented to be present. The spectacle which they then witnessed was voted most agreeable. The bulls, which turned out to be heifers, very lithe and excitable, were housed in boxed stalls, which bore their respective names: Isabel, Rosa, Paquita, Adelaide, Carlota and Sofia. The ring itself was an improvised arrangement constructed in a great racquet court. The spectators, according to their means, found seats on either side, the poorer in the sun and the more wealthy in the shaded Tribune d'Honneur. After a premonitory blare from municipal brass the quadrille entered the arena. They were a good-looking set of men, more plainly dressed than their bloodier brothers of Spain, and very agile. Two of them carrying long poles stationed themselves at the sides, one, armed with a barb laid himself down a few feet from Isabel's door, and a fourth threw his soft hat in the middle of the ring, put his feet in it and stood expectant. In a moment a latch was drawn, Isabel leaped from her stall, bounded over the prostrate form that pricked her on her way and made a straight rush for the motionless figure in the centre of the ring. When she reached him he was in the air and over her with his feet still in the hat. Isabel was bewildered, instead of goring a man she had run her horns into empty space and in her annoyance she turned viciously at one of the pole-bearing gentlemen who vaulted over her as easily as were he crossing a gutter, but in vaulting the pole slipped from him, and amid the applause of the audience Isabel chased him across the ring to a high fence opposite, and to which he rose like a bird with Isabel's horns on his heels. There was more of this amusement, and then Isabel, a trifle tired, was lured back to her box; Rosa was loosed and the performance repeated.

The escapes seemed so hairbreadth that Mr. Blydenburg announced his intention of witnessing a genuine bull fight, and on the way to Saint Jean urged his companions to accompany him over the border and view the real article. "There is one announced for next Sunday," he said, "at San Sebastian, a stone's throw from here." The appetite of all had been whetted, and during the rest of the drive, Mr. Blydenburg discoursed on the subject with such learning and enthusiasm that even his daughter consented to forget her Sabbath principles and make one of the projected party.

When the meal was done, they went into the toy Casino. There was a band playing at one end of the hall, the which was so narrow that the director had been obliged to select thin musicians, and beyond was a paperless reading-room, a vague café, a dwarf theatre, and a salle-de-jeu in white and gamboge. In the latter division, where the high life of Saint Jean had assembled, stood a table that resembled a roulette. In its centre were miniature revolving bulls, which immediately attracted Mr. Blydenburg's attention, and on the green baize were painted the names of cities.

"Banderilla! Ruego! Sevilla!" the croupier called, as the party entered. In one hand he held a rake, with which he possessed himself of the stakes of those who had lost, and with the other hand he tossed out coin to those who had won. The machinery was again set in motion, and when the impulse had ceased to act he called out anew, "Espada! Nero! Madrid!"

Mr. Blydenburg was thoroughly interested. In the residue of twenty-five French lessons, which he had learned in his boyhood from a German, he made bold to demand information.

"It's the neatest game in the world," the croupier replied; "six for one on the cities, even on the colors, even on banderilla or espada, and twenty for one on Frascuelo." And, as he gave the latter information, he pointed to a little figure armed with a sword, which was supposed to represent that famous matador. "The minimum," he added, obligingly, "is fifty centimes; the maximum, forty sous."

"I'll go Frascuelo," said Blydenburg, and suiting the action to the word, he placed a coin on the table. Maida, meanwhile, had put money on everything—cities, colors, banderilla, espada, and Frascuelo as well. To the surprise of every one, but most to that of the croupier, Frascuelo won. Maida saw twenty francs swept from her and forty returned. Blydenburg, who had played a closer game, received forty also, but he lost nothing, and he beamed as joyously as had the University of Copenhagen crowned an essay of his own manufacture.

It was by means of these mild amusements that the first week of their sojourn was helped away. Through the kindness of an international acquaintance, Mr. Incoul had been made welcome at the Cercle de Biarritz, and in that charming summer club, where there is much high play and perfect informality, he had become acquainted with a Spaniard, the Marquis of Zunzarraga.

One day when the latter gentleman had wearied of the columns of the *Epoca* and Mr. Incoul, and sought in vain for some refreshment from *Galignani*, they drew their chairs together and exchanged cigarettes.

In answer to the question which is addressed to every new-comer, Mr. Incoul expressed himself pleased with the country, adding that were not hotel life always distasteful he would be glad to remain on indefinitely.

"You might take a villa," the marquis suggested. To this Mr. Incoul made no reply. The nobleman fluttered his fingers a moment and then said, "take mine, you can have it, servants and all."

The Villa Zunzarraga was near the hotel and its airy architecture had already attracted Mr. Incoul's eye. It was a modern improvement on a feudal château, there were turreted wings in which the machicoulis were replaced by astragals and a broad and double stairway of marble led up to the main entrance.

"If you have nothing better to do to-day," the marquis continued, "go in and take a look at it. I have never rented it before, but this summer the marquesa is with the queen, my mistress, and I would be glad to have it off my hands."

After consulting Maida in regard to her wishes, Mr. Incoul determined to act on the suggestion, and that afternoon they went together to view the villa. In its appointments there was little fault to be found. There was no vestibule, unless, indeed, the entrance hall, which was large enough to accommodate a small cotillon, could be so considered; on the right were reception-rooms, to the left a dining-room, all facing the sea, while at the rear, overlooking a quiet garden that seemed to extend indefinitely and lose itself in the lilac fringes of the tamaris, was a library. On the floor above were bed and sitting rooms. In one wing were the offices, kitchen and servants' quarters, in another was the coach-house and stables.

Under the guidance of the host, Mr. Incoul went to explore the place, while Maida remained in the library. It was a satisfactory room, lined on three sides with low, well-filled book-cases, the windows were doors and extended nearly to the ceiling, but the light fell through pink awnings under which was a verandah, with steps that led to the garden below. From the walls hung selections of Goya's Proverbios and Tauromaquia, a series of nightmares in black and white. Among them was a picture of a lake of blood haunted by evil spirits; a vertiginous flight of phantoms more horrible than any Doré ever saw; a reunion of sorcerers with cats for steeds; women tearing teeth from the mouths of the gibbeted; a confusion of demons and incubes; a disordered dance of delirious manolas; caricatures that held the soul of Hoffmann; the disembowelment of fantastic chulos; horses tossed by bulls with chimerical horns; but best of all, a skeleton leaning with a leer from the tomb and scrawling on it the significant legend, *Nada*, nothing.

In one corner, on a pedestal, there glittered a Buddha, the legs crossed and a smile of indolent apathy on its imbecile features. Behind it was a giant crucifix with arms outstretched like the wings of woe.

Maida wandered from book-case to book-case, examining the contents with incurious eye. The titles were strange to her and new. In one division were the works of Archilaus, Albert le Grand, Raymond Lulle, Armand de Villenova, Nostradamus, and Paracelsus, the masters of occult science. Another was given up to Spanish literature. There were the poems of Berceo, the romancero of the church; the codex of Alphonso X., the Justinian of mediæval Spain; El Tesoro, a work on alchemy by the same royal hand and the Conquista d'ultramar. There was the Libro de consejos, by Sanchez IV.; and Bicerro, the armorial of the nobility, by his son, Alphonso XI. Therewith was a collection of verse of the troubadours, the songs of Aimeric de Bellinsi, Foulque de Lunel, Carbonel, Nat de Tours, and Riquier, the last of the knight-errants. Then came the poems of Juan de Mena, the Dante of Castille; the Rabelaisian relaxations of the Archbishop of Hita; the cancionero of Ausias March, that of Baena, of Stuñiga, and that of Ixar.

Another book-case was filled with the French poets, from Villon to Soulary. The editions were delicious, a pleasure to hold, and many of them bore the imprint of Lemerre. Among them was the Fleurs du Mal, an unexpurgated copy, and by it were the poems of Baudelaire's decadent descendants, Paul Verlaine and Mallarmé.

There were other book-cases, and of these there was one of which the door was locked. In it were Justine and Juliette, by the Marquis de Sade; the works of Piron; the works of Beroalde de Verville; a copy of Mercius; a copy of Thérèse Philosophe; the De Arcanis Amoris; Mirabeau's Rideau levé; Gamaini, by Alfred de Musset and George Sand; Boccaccio; the Heptameron; Paphian Days; Crébillon's Sopha; the Erotika Biblion; the Satyricon of Petronius; an illustrated catalogue of the Naples Museum; Voltaire's Pucelle; a work or two of Diderot's; Maiseroy's Deux Amies; the Clouds; the Curée; everything, in fact, from Aristophanes to Zola.

The collection was meaningless to Maida, and she turned aside and went out on the verandah. Below, on the gravel walk, was a cat with a tail like a banner, and a neck furred like a ruff. Maida crumpled a bit of paper and threw it down. The cat jumped at it at once, toyed with it for a moment, and then, sliding backwards with a crab-like movement, its back arched, and its ears drawn down, it caught a glimpse of Maida's unfamiliar figure, and fled to the bushes with a shriek of feigned terror. A servant passed, and ignorant of Maida's presence, apostrophized the retreating feline as a loafer and a liar.

A moment later Mr. Incoul and the marquis reappeared.

"I have been admiring your Angora," Maida said, "but I fear I startled it."

The marquis rubbed his hands together thoughtfully. "It is a wonderful animal," he answered, "but it is not an Angora, it is a Thibetian cat, and though it does not talk, at least it converses. It is so odd in its ways that I called it Mistigris, as one might a familiar spirit, but my children prefer Ti-Mi; they think it more Thibetian, I fancy." He coughed slightly and looking at the points of his fingers, he added, "I will leave it with you of course."

And then Maida understood that the matter was settled and that the house was hers.

CHAPTER VII.
WHAT MAY BE SEEN FROM A PALCO.

The installation was accomplished without difficulty. The marquis migrated to other shores and it took Maida but a short time to discover the pleasures of being luxuriously housed. The apartment which she selected for herself was composed of four rooms; there was a sitting-room in an angle with windows overlooking the sea and others that gave on a quiet street which skirted one wing of the villa. Next to it was a bed-room also overlooking the street, while back of that, on the garden side, was a bath and a dressing-room. A wide hall that was like a haunt of echoes separated these rooms from those of her husband.

Through the street, which was too steep to be much of a thoroughfare, there came each morning the clinging strain of a pastoral melody, and a pipe-playing goat-herd would pass leading his black, long-haired flock to the doors of those who bought the milk. When he had gone the silence was stirred by another sound, a call that rose and fell with exquisite sweetness and died away in infinite vibrations: it came from a little old woman, toothless and bent, who, with summer in her voice, hawked crisp gold bread of crescent shape, vaunting its delicacy in birdlike trills. There were other venders who announced their wares in similar ways, and one, a fisher, chaunted a low and mournful measure which he must have caught from the sea.

It was pleasant to be waked in this wise, Maida thought, and as she lay in her great bed of odorous wood, she listened to the calls, and when they had passed, the boom and retreating rustle of the waves occupied and lulled her. In such moments the thoughts that visited her were impermanent and fleeting. She made no effort to stay them, preferring the vague to the outlined, watching the changes and transformations of fancy as though her soul and she were separate, as were her mind a landscape, some

Paysage choisi,
Que vont charmant masques et bergamasques
Jouant du luth et dansant et quasi
Tristes sous leurs déguisements fantasques.

The room was an accomplice of her languor. The windows were curtained with filmy yellow. Before them were miniature balconies filled with flowers, and as the sun rose the light filtered through flesh-colored awnings striated with ochre. The floor was a mosaic of variegated and lacquered wood. On either side of the bed were silk rugs, sea green and pink, seductive to the foot; the ceiling was a summer sky at dawn, a fresco in cinnabar and smalt.

The Blydenburgs, less luxuriously inclined, remained at the hotel. Mr. Blydenburg had not as yet enjoyed an opportunity of conversing in Basque; he had indeed attempted to address a mildewed little girl whom he encountered one day when loitering on the cliffs, but the child had taken flight, and a mule that was pasturing on a bramble, threw back its ears, elongated its tail and curving its lips, brayed with such anguish that Mr. Blydenburg was fain to delay his studies until fortune offered a more favorable opportunity.

It was at San Sebastian, he thought, that such an opportunity would be found ready made, and on the morning of the projected excursion he was in great and expectant spirits.

The morning itself was one of those delicious forenoons that reminded one of Veronese. In the air was a caress and in the breeze an exhilaration and a tonic. In the streets and about the squares there was an unusual liveliness, much loud talking, a great many oaths, and the irritation and excitement which is the prelude to a festival. The entire summer colony seemed to be on its way to Spain.

In the court-yard of the Villa Zunzarraga four horses harnessed to a landau stood in readiness. On the box the driver glistened with smart buttons and silver braid. His coat was short, his culottes were white, his waistcoat red, and he had made himself operatic with the galloons and trappings of an eighteenth-century postilion. It was not every day in the year that he drove to a corrida. By way of preparation for the coming spectacle, Karl, who stood at the carriage door, had already engaged a palco.

When Blydenburg and Milly arrived, and the party had entered the landau, there was a brisk drive through the town and a long sweep down the Route d'Espagne than which even the Corniche is not more lovely. The vaporous Pyrenees seemed near enough to be in reach of the hand, the elms that lined the roadside were monstrous, like the elms in a Druid forest, the fields were as green as had they been painted. There were pink villas with blinds of pale yellow, white houses roofed with tiles of mottled red, gardens splendid with the scent of honeysuckle, and children, bright-eyed, clear-featured, devoured by vermin and greed, ran out in a bold, aggressive way and called for coin.

"*Estamos en España!*" The carriage had come to a sudden halt. In the beauties of the landscape the journey had been forgotten. But at the driver's word there came to each of them that sudden thrill which visits every one that crosses a new frontier. Blydenburg looked eagerly about him. He had expected to be greeted by alcaldes and alguacils, he had fancied that he would view a jota, or at the very least a roadside bolero. "Are we really in Spain?" he wondered. In places of ladies in mantillas and short skirts there was a group of mangy laborers, the alcaldes and alguacils were represented by a sullen aduenaro, and the only trace of local color was in a muttered *"Coño de Dios"* that came wearily from a bystander. Certainly they were in Spain.

The custom-house officer made a motion, and the carriage swept on. To the left was Fuenterrabia, dozing on its gulf of blue, and soon they were in Irun. There was another halt for lunch and a change of horses, and then, on again. The scenery grew wilder, and the carriage jolted, for the road was poor. They passed the Jayzquibel, the Gaïnchurisqueta, the hamlet of Lezo, Passaje, from whence Lafayette set sail; Renteria, a city outside of the year of our Lord; they crossed the Oyarzun, they passed Alza, another stream was bridged and at last the circus hove in sight.

The bull-ring of San Sebastian is sufficiently vast for a battalion to manœuvre in at its ease. It is circled by a barrier some five feet high, back of which is another and a higher one. Between the two is a narrow passage. Above the higher barrier rise the tendidos—the stone benches of the amphitheatre—slanting upwards until they reach a gallery, in which are the gradas—the wooden benches—and directly over these, on the flooring above, are the palcos or boxes. Each box holds twenty people. They are all alike save that of the President's, which is larger, decorated with hangings and furnished with chairs, the other boxes having only seats of board. Under the President's box, and beneath the tendidos, is the toril from which the bulls are loosed. Opposite, across the arena, is the matedero, the gateway through which the horses enter and the dead are dragged out. In the passage between the two barriers are stationed the "supes," who cover up the blood, unsaddle dead horses, and attend to other matters of a similar and agreeable nature. There, too, the carpenters stand ready to repair any injury to the woodwork, and among them is a man in black, who at times issues furtively and gives a *coup de grace* to a writhing beast. There also are usually a few privileged amateurs who seek that vantage ground much as the dilettanti seek the side scenes of the theatre.

These arrangements, which it takes a paragraph to describe, are absorbed at a glance, but with that glance there comes an aftershock—a riot of color that would take a library to convey. For the moment the eye is dazzled; a myriad of multicolored fans are fluttering like fabulous butterflies; there are unimagined combinations of insolent hues; a multitude of rainbows oscillating in a deluge of light. And while the eye is dazzled the ear is bewildered, the pulse is stirred. The excitement of ten thousand people is contagious; the uproar is as deafening as the thunder of cannon. And then, at once, almost without transition, a silence. The President has come, and the most magnificent of modern spectacles is about to begin.

Almost simultaneously with the appearance of the chief magistrate of the town, the Incouls and Blydenburgs entered their box. There was a blast from a trumpet and an official in the costume known as that of Henri IV. issued on horseback from the matedero. The ring which a moment before had been peopled with amateurs was emptied in a trice. The principal actor, the espada, Mazzantini, escorted by his cuadrilla and followed by the picadors, advanced to the centre of the arena and there amid an explosion of bravos, bowed with a grace like that which Talma must have possessed, first to the President, who raised his high hat in return, and then in circular wise to the spectators.

He was young and exceedingly handsome, blue of eye and clear-featured; he smiled in the contented way of one who is sure of his own powers, and the applause redoubled. The Basques have made a national idol of him, for by birth he is one of them and very popular in Guipuzcoa. He was dressed after the fashion of Figaro in the "Barbiere," his knee breeches were of vermilion silk seamed with a broad spangle, his stockings were of flesh color, he wore a short, close-fitting jacket, richly embroidered; the vest was very low but gorgeous with designs; about his waist was a scarlet sash; his shoulders were heavy with gold and on his head was a black pomponed turban, the torero variety of the Tam O'Shanter. His costume had been imitated by the chulos and banderilleros. Nothing more seductive could be imagined. They were all of them slight, lithe and agile, and behind them the picadors in the Moorish splendor of their dress looked like giants on horseback.

The President dropped from his box the key of the toril. The alguacil is supposed to catch it in his hat, but in this instance he muffed it; it was picked up by another; the alguacil fled from the ring, the picadors stationed themselves lance in hand at equal distances about the barrier, the chulos prepared their mantles, there was a ringing fanfare, the doors of the toril flew open, and a black monster with the colors of his *ganaderia* fastened to his neck shot into the arena.

If he hesitated no one knew it. There was a confused mass of horse, bull and man, he was away again, another picador was down, and then attracted by the waving cloak of a chulo he turned and chased it across the ring. The chulo was over the fence in a second, and the bull rose like a greyhound and crossed it, too. Truly a magnificent beast. The supes and amateurs were in the ring in an instant and back again when the bull had passed. A door was opened, and surging again into the ring he swept like an avalanche on a picador, and raising him horse and all into the air flung him down as it seemed into the very pits of death. The picador was under the horse and the bull's horns were seeking him, but the brute reckoned without the espada. Mazzantini had caught him by the tail, which he twisted in such exquisite fashion that he was fain to turn, and as he turned the espada turned with him. The chulos meanwhile raised the picador over the barrier, for his legs and loins were so heavy with iron that once down he could not rise unassisted. Across the arena a horse lay quivering in a bath of gore, his feet entangled in his entrails, and another, unmounted, staggered along dyeing the sand with zigzags of the blood that spouted, fountain-like, from his breast. And over all was the tender blue of the sky of Spain.

When Mazzantini loosed his hold, he stood a moment, folded his arms, gave the bull a glance of contempt, turned on his heel and sauntered away. The applause was such as no *cabotin* has ever received. It was the delirious plaudits of ten thousand people drunk with the sun, with excitement—intoxicated with blood. Mazzantini bowed as calmly as were he a tenor, whose *ut de poitrine* had found appreciation in the stalls. And while the applause still lasted, the bull caught the staggering, blindfolded, unprotected horse and tossed him sheer over the barrier, and would have jumped after him had he not perceived a fourth picador ambling cautiously with pointed lance. At him he made a fresh rush, but the picador's lance was in his neck and held him away. He broke loose, however, and with an under lunge disemboweled the shuddering horse.

There was another blast of the trumpets, the signal for the banderilleros whose office it is to plant barbs in the neck of the bull—a delicate operation, for the banderillero must face the bull, and should he trip he is dead. This ceremony is seldom performed until the bull shows signs of weariness; then the barbs act like a tonic. In this instance the bull seemed as fresh as were he on his native heath, and the spectators were clamorous in their indignation. They called for more horses; they accused the management of economy; men stood up and shook their fists at the President; it was for him to order out fresh steeds, and, as he sat impassible, *pollice verso*, as one may say, they shouted "*Fuego al presidente, perro de presidente*"—dog of a president; set him on fire. And there were cat-calls and the screech of tin horns, and resounding and noisy insults, until the general attention was diverted by the pose of the banderillas and the leaping and kicking of the bull, seeking to free his neck from the torturing barbs. At last, when he had been punctured eight times, he sought the centre of the ring, and stood there almost motionless, his tufted tail swaying nervously, his tongue lolling from his mouth, a mist of vapor circling from his nostrils, seething about his splendid horns and wrinkled neck, and in his great eyes a look of wonder, as though amazed that men could be crueler than he.

Again the trumpets sounded. Mazzantini, with a sword concealed in a muleta of bright scarlet silk, and accompanied by the chulos, approached him. The chulos flaunted their vivid cloaks, and when the bull, roused by the hated colors to new indignation, turned to chase them, they slipped aside and in the centre of the ring stood a young man dressed as airily as a dancer in a ballet, in a costume that a pin would have perforated, and before him a maddened and a gigantic brute.

In a second the bull was on him, but in that second a tongue of steel leaped from the muleta, glittered like a silver flash in the air, and straight over the lowered horns it swept and then cleaved down through the parting flesh and touched the spring of life. At the very feet of the espada the bull fell; he had not lost a drop of blood; it was the supreme expression of tauromaquia, the recognition that skill works from force.

And then the applause! There was a whirl of hats and cigars and cigarettes, and had San Sabastian been richer there would have been a shower of coin. Women kissed their hands and men held out their arms to embrace him. It was the delirium of appreciation. And Mazzantini saluted and bowed and smiled. He was quite at home, and calmer and more tranquil than any spectator. Suddenly there was a rush of caparisoned mules, ropes were attached to the dead horses, the bull was dragged out, the blood was concealed with sand, the toilet of the ring was made, the trumpets sounded and the last act of the first of the wonderful cycle of dramas was done.

There were five more bulls to be killed that day, but with their killing the action with which these pages have to deal need not be further delayed. From the box in the sombra Mr. Incoul had watched the spectacle with unemotional curiosity. Blydenburg, who had fortified himself with the contents of a pocket flask, manifested his earliest delight by shouting Bravo, but with such a disregard of the first syllable, and such an explosion of the second, that Mr. Incoul mistaking the applause for an imitation of the bark of a dog had at last begged him to desist.

The adjoining box was crowded, and among the occupants was a delicious young girl, with the Orient in her eyes, and lips that said Drink me. To her the spectacle was evidently one of alluring pathos. *"Pobre caballo,"* she would murmur when a horse fell, and then with her fan she would hide the bridge of her nose as though that were her organ of vision. But no matter how high the fan might be raised she always managed to see, and with the seeing there came from her compassionate little noises, a mingling of *"ay"* and *"Dios mio,"* that was most agreeable to listen to. Miss Blydenburg, who sat so near her that she might have touched her elbow, took these little noises for signals and according to their rise and fall learned when and when not to look down into the terrible ring below.

In the momentary intermission that occurred after the duel between the espada and the first bull, a mozo, guided by Karl, appeared in the box bearing with him cool liquids from the caverns beneath. Blydenburg, whose throat was parched with brandy and the strain of his incessant shouts, swallowed a naranjada at a gulp. Mr. Incoul declined to take anything, but the ladies found much refreshment in a concoction of white almonds which affects the tonsils as music affects the ear.

It was not until this potion had been absorbed that Maida began to take any noticeable interest. She had been fatigued by the drive, enervated by the heat, and the noise and clamor was certainly not in the nature of a sedative. But the almonds brought her comfort. She changed her seat from the rear of the box to the front, and sat with one arm on the balustrade, her hand supporting her delicate chin, and as her eyes followed the prowess of the bull she looked like some fair Pasiphae in modern guise.

It must have been the novelty of the scene that interested her. The light, the unusual and brilliant costumes, the agility of the actors, and the wonder of the sky, entered, probably, as component parts into any pleasure that she experienced. Certainly it could have been nothing else, for she was quick to avert her eyes whenever blood seemed imminent. The second bull, however, was far less active than the first. He had indeed accomplished a certain amount of destruction, but his attacks were more perfunctory than angered, and it was not until he had been irritated by the colored barbs that he displayed any lively sense of resentment. Then one of the banderilleros showed himself either awkward or timid; he may have been both; in any event his success was slight, and as the Spanish audience is not indulgent, he was hissed and hooted at. "Give him a pistol," cried some—the acmé of sarcasm—"*Torero de las marinas*," cried others. He was offered a safe seat in the tendidos. One group adjured the President to order his instant imprisonment. One might have thought that the tortures of the Inquisition could not be too severe for such a lout as he.

Maida, who was ignorant of the duties of a banderillero, looked down curiously at the gesticulating crowd below. The cause of their indignation she was unable to discover, and was about to turn to Mr. Blydenburg for information, when there came a singing in her ears. The question passed unuttered from her thoughts. The ring, the people, the sky itself had vanished. Near the toril, on a bench of stone, was Lenox Leigh.

CHAPTER VIII.
AN UNEXPECTED GUEST.

Gradually the whirling ceased, the singing left her ears. Leigh raised his hat and Maida bowed in return. His eyes lingered on her a moment, and then he turned and disappeared.

"A friend of mine, Mr. Leigh, is down there," the girl announced. Her husband looked over the rail. "He's gone," she added. "I fancy he is coming up here."

"Who's coming?" Blydenburg inquired, for he had caught the words.

"A friend of my wife's," Mr. Incoul answered. "A man named Leigh—do you know him?"

"Mrs. Manhattan's brother, isn't he? No, I don't know him, but Milly does, I think. Don't you, Milly?"

Milly waved her head vaguely. She indeed knew the young man in question, but she was not over-confident that he had ever been more than transiently aware of her maidenly existence. She had, however, no opportunity to formulate her uncertainty in words. There was a rap on the door and Leigh entered.

Mr. Incoul rose as becomes a host. The young man bowed collectively to him and the Blydenburgs. He touched Maida's hand and found a seat behind her. A bull-fight differs from an opera in many things, but particularly in this, that there may be exclamations, but there is no attempt at continuous conversation. Lenox Leigh, though not one to whom custom is law, said little during the rest of the performance. Now and then he bent forward to Maida, but whatever he may have said his remarks were fragmentary and casual. This much Miss Blydenburg noticed, and she noticed also that Maida appeared more interested in her glove than in the spectacle in the ring.

When the sixth and last bull had been vanquished and the crowd was leaving the circus, Mr. Incoul turned to his guest, "We are to dine at the Inglaterra, will you not join us?"

"Thank you," Lenox answered, "I shall be glad to. I came here in the train and I have had nothing since morning. I have been ravenous for hours, so much so," he added lightly, "that I have been trying to poison my hunger by thinking of the dishes that I dislike the most, beer soup, for instance, stewed snails, carp cooked in sweetmeats or unseasoned salads of cactus hearts."

"I don't know," Mr. Incoul answered gravely. "I don't know what we will have to-night. The dinner was ordered last week. They may have cooked it then."

"Possibly they did. On a *fiesta* San Sebastian is impossible. There are seven thousand strangers here to-day and the accommodations are insufficient for a third of them."

"I want to know—" exclaimed Blydenburg, always anxious for information. They had moved out of the box and aided by the crowd were drifting slowly down the stair.

At the *salida* Karl stood waiting to conduct them to the carriage.

"If you will get in with the ladies," said Mr. Incoul, "Blydenburg and myself will walk. The hotel can't be far."

To this proposal the young man objected. He had been sitting all day, he explained, and preferred to stretch his legs. He may have had other reasons, but if he had he said nothing of them. At once, then, it was arranged that the ladies, under Karl's protection, should drive to the Inglaterra, and that the others should follow on foot.

Half an hour later the entire party were seated at a table overlooking the Concha. The sun had sunk into the ocean as though it were imbibing an immense blue syrup. On either side of the bay rose miniature mountains, Orgullo and Igueldo tiara'd with fortresses and sloped with green. To the right in the distance was a great unfinished casino, and facing it, beneath Orgullo, was a cluster of white ascending villas. The dusk was sudden. The sky after hesitating between salmon and turquoise had chosen a lapis lazuli, which it changed to indigo, and with that for flooring the stars came out and danced.

The dinner passed off very smoothly. In spite of his boasted hunger, Lenox ate but sparingly. He was frugal as a Spaniard, and in the expansion which the heavy wine of the country will sometimes cause, Mr. Blydenburg declared that he looked like one. Each of the party had his or her little say about the corrida and its emotions, and Blydenburg, after discoursing with much learning on the subject, declared, to whomsoever would listen, that for his part he regretted the gladiators of Rome. As a topic, the bull fight was inexhaustible. Every thread of conversation led back to it, and necessarily, in the course of the meal, Lenox was asked how it was that he happened to be present.

"I arrived at Biarritz from Paris last night," he explained, "and when I learned this morning that there was to be a bull-fight, I was not in a greater hurry to do anything else than to buy a ticket and take the train."

"Was it crowded?" Blydenburg asked in his florid way.

"Rather. It was comfortable enough till we reached Irun, but there I got out for a Spanish cigar, and when I returned, the train was so packed that I was obliged to utilize a first-class ticket in a third-class car. None of the people who lunched at the buffet were able to get back. I suppose three hundred were left. There was almost a riot. The station-master said that Irun was the head of the line, and to reserve a seat one must sit in it. Of course those who had seats were hugely amused at those who had none. One man, a Frenchman, bullied the station-master dreadfully. He said it was every kind of an outrage; that he ought to put on more cars; that he was incompetent; that he was imbecile; that he didn't know his business. 'It's the law,' said the station-master. 'I don't care that for your law!' cried the Frenchman. 'But the Préfet, sir.' 'To blazes with your Préfet!' But that was too strong. The Frenchman might abuse what he saw fit, but the Préfet evidently was sacred. I suppose it was treasonable to speak of him in that style. In any event, the station-master called up a file of soldiers and had the Frenchman led away. The on-lookers were simply frantic with delight. If the Frenchman had only been shot before their eyes it would indeed have been a charming prelude to a bull fight." And then with an air that suggested retrospects of unexpressed regret, he added pensively, "I have never seen a man shot."

"No?" said Milly, boldly; "no more have I. Not that I want to, though," she hastened to explain. "It must be horrid."

Lenox looked up at her and then his eyes wandered to Maida, and rested caressingly in her own. But the caress was transient. Immediately he turned and busied himself with his plate.

"Are you to be in Biarritz long?" Mr. Incoul asked. The tone was perfectly courteous, friendly, even, but at the moment from the very abruptness of the question Lenox feared that the caress had been intercepted and something of the mute drama divined. Mentally he arranged Mr. Incoul as one constantly occupied in repeating *J'ai de bon tabac, tu n'en auras pas*, and it was his design to disarm that gentleman of any suspicion he might harbor that his good tobacco, in this instance at least, was an envied possession or one over which he would be called to play the sentinel. The rôle of *mari sage* was frequent enough on the Continent, but few knew better than Lenox Leigh that it is rarely enacted in the States, and his intuitions had told him long before that it was one for which Mr. Incoul was ill adapted. Yet between the *mari sage* and the suspicionless husband there is a margin, and it was on that margin that Lenox determined that Mr. Incoul should tread. "No," he answered at once, and without any visible sign of preoccupation. "No, a day or two at most; I am on my way to Andalucia."

Blydenburg, as usual, was immediately interested. "It's very far, isn't it?" he panted.

"Not so far as it used to be. Nowadays one can go all the way in a sleeping car. Gautier, who discovered it, had to go in a stage-coach, which must have been tedious. But in spite of the railways the place is pretty much the same as it has been ever since the Middle Ages. Even the cholera has been unable to banish the local color. There are trains in Seville precisely as there are steamboats on the Grand Canal. But the sky is the same, and in the Sierra Morena there are still Moors and as yet no advertisements."

"You have been there then?"

"Yes, I was there some years ago. You ought to go yourself. I know of nothing so fabulous in its beauty. It is true I was there in the spring, but the autumn ought not to be a bad time to go. The country is parched perhaps, but then you would hardly camp out."

"What do you say, Incoul?" Blydenburg asked. "Wouldn't you like it?" he inquired of Maida.

"I could tell better when we get there," she answered; "but we might go," she added, looking at her husband.

"Why," said Blydenburg, "we could see Madrid and Burgos and Valladolid. It's all in the way."

Lenox interrupted him. "They are tiresome cities though, and gloomy to a degree. Valladolid and Burgos are like congeries of deserted prisons, Madrid is little different from any other large city. Fuenterrabia, next door here, is a thousand times more interesting. It is Cordova you should visit and Ronda and Granada and Sevilla and Cadix." And, as he uttered the names of these cities, he aromatized each of them with an accent that threw Blydenburg into stupors of admiration. Pronounced in that way they seemed worth visiting indeed.

"Which of them do you like the best?"

"I liked them all," Lenox answered. "I liked each of them best."

"But which is the most beautiful?"

"That depends on individual taste. I prefer Ronda, but Grenada, I think, is most admired. If you will let me, I will quote a high authority:

"'Grenade efface en tout ses rivales; Grenade
Chante plus mollement la molle sérénade;
Elle peint ses maisons des plus riches couleurs,
Et l'on dit, que les vents suspendent leurs haleines,

Quand, par un soir d'été, Grenade dans ses plaines,
Répand ses femmes et ses fleurs.'"

In private life, verse is difficult of recitation, but Lenox recited well. He made such music of the second line that there came with his voice the sound of guitars; the others he delivered with the vowels full as one hears them at the Comédie, and therewith was a little pantomime so explanatory and suggestive that Blydenburg, whose knowledge of French was of the most rudimentary description, understood it all, and, in consequence, liked the young man the better.

The dinner was done, and they moved out on the terrace. The moon had chased the stars, the Concha glittered with lights, and before the hotel a crowd circled in indolent coils as though wearied with the holiday. There were many people, too, on the terrace, and in passing from the dining-room the little party, either by accident or design, got cut in twain. For the first time since the spring evening, Maida and Lenox were alone. Their solitude, it is true, was public, but that mattered little.

Maida utilized the earliest moment by asking her companion how he got there. "You should not have spoken to me," she added, before he could have answered.

"Maida!"

"No, you must go, you—"

"But I only came to find you," he whispered.

"To find me? How did you know where I was?"

"The *Morning News* told me. I was in Paris, on my way to Baden, for I heard you were there, and then, of course, when I saw in the paper that you were here, I followed after."

"Then you are not going to Andalucia?"

"No, not unless you do."

The girl wrung her hand. "Oh, Lenox, do go away!"

"I can't, nor do you wish it. You must let me see you. I will come to you to-morrow—he has an excellent voice, not so full as Gayarré's, but his method is better."

Mr. Incoul had suddenly approached them, and as suddenly Lenox's tone had changed. To all intents and purposes he was relating the merits of a tenor.

"The carriage is here," said Maida's husband, "we must be going; I am sorry we can't offer you a seat, Mr. Leigh, we are a trifle crowded as it is."

"Thank you, you are very kind. The train will take me safely enough."

He walked with them to the carriage, and aided Maida to enter it. Karl, who had been standing at the door, mounted to the box. When all were seated, Mr. Incoul added: "You must come and see us."

"Yes, come and see us, too," Blydenburg echoed. "By the way, where are you stopping?"

"I shall be glad to do so," Lenox answered; "I am at the Grand." He raised his hat and wished them a pleasant drive. The moon was shining full in his face, and Miss Blydenburg thought him even handsomer than Mazzantini. His good wishes were answered in chorus, Karl nudged the driver, and in a moment the carriage swept by and left him standing in the road.

"What a nice, frank fellow he is," Blydenburg began; "so different from the general run of young New Yorkers. There, I forgot to tell him I knew his sister; I am sorry, it would have seemed sort of friendly, made him feel more at home, don't you think? Not but that he seemed perfectly at his ease as it was. I wonder why he doesn't marry? None of those Leighs have money, have they? He could pick up an heiress, though, in no time, if he wanted to. Perhaps he prefers to be a bachelor. If he does I don't blame him a bit, a good-looking young fellow—"

And so the amiable gentleman rambled on. After a while finding that the reins of conversation were solely in his own hands, he took the fullest advantage of his position and discoursed at length on the bull fight, its history, its possibilities, the games of the Romans, how they fared under the Goths, what improvements came with the Moors, and wound up by suggesting an immediate visit to Fuenterrabia.

For the moment no enthusiasm was manifested. Mr. Incoul admitted that he would like to go, but the ladies said nothing, and presently the two men planned a little excursion by themselves.

Miss Blydenburg had made herself comfortable and fallen into a doze, but Maida sat watching the retreating uplands with unseeing eyes. Her thoughts had wandered, the visible was lost to her. Who knows what women see or the dreams and regrets that may come to the most matter-of-fact? Not long ago at the opera, in a little Italian town, the historian noticed an old lady, one who looked anything but sentimental, for that matter rather fierce than otherwise, but who, when Cherubino had sung his enchanting song, brushed away a furtive and unexpected tear. *Voi che sapete* indeed! Perhaps to her own cost she had learned and was grieving dumbly then over some ashes that the strain had stirred, and it is not impossible that as Maida sat watching the retreating uplands her own thoughts had circled back to an earlier summer when first she learned what Love might be.

CHAPTER IX.
MR. INCOUL DINES IN SPAIN.

On the morrow Mr. Blydenburg consulted his guide-books. The descriptions of Fuenterrabia were vague but alluring. The streets, he learned, were narrow; the roofs met; the houses were black with age; the doors were heavy with armorials; the windows barred—in short, a mediæval burg that slept on a blue gulf and let Time limp by unmarked. Among the inhabitants were some, he found, who accommodated travelers. The inns, it is true, were unstarred, but the names were so rich in suggestion that the neglect was not noticed. Mr. Blydenburg had never passed a night in Spain, and he felt that he would like to do so. This desire he succeeded in awakening in Mr. Incoul, and together they agreed to take an afternoon train, explore the town, pass the evening at the Casino and return to Biarritz the next morning. The programme thus arranged was put into immediate execution; two days after the bull fight they were again on their way to the frontier, and, as the train passed out of the station on its southern journey, Maida and Lenox Leigh were preparing for a stroll on the sands.

There is at Biarritz a division of the shore which, starting from the ruins of a corsair's castle, extends on to Saint-Jean-de-Luz. It is known as the Côte des Basques. On one side are the cliffs, on the other the sea, and between the two is a broad avenue which almost disappears when the tide is high. The sand is fine as face powder, *nuance* Rachel, packed hard. From the cliffs the view is delicious: in the distance are the mountains curving and melting in the haze; below, the ocean, spangled at the edges, is of a milky blue. Seen from the shore, the sea has the color of absinthe, an opalescent green, entangled and fringed with films of white; here the mountains escape in the perspective, and as the sun sinks the cliffs glitter. At times the sky is flecked with little clouds that dwindle and fade into spirals of pink; at others great masses rise sheer against the horizon, as might the bastions of Titan homes; and again are gigantic cathedrals, their spires lost in azure, their turrets swooning in excesses of vermilion grace. The only sound is from the waves, but few come to listen. The Côte des Basques is not fashionable with the summer colony; it is merely beautiful and solitary.

It was on the downs that Maida and Lenox first chose to walk, but after a while a sloping descent invited them to the shore below. Soon they rounded a projecting cliff, and Biarritz was hidden from them. The background was chalk festooned with green; afar were the purple outlines of the Pyrenees, and before them the ocean murmured its temptations of couch and of tomb.

They had been talking earnestly with the egotism of people to whom everything save self is landscape. The encircling beauty in which they walked had not left them unimpressed, yet the influence had been remote and undiscerned; the effect had been that of accessories. But now they were silent, for the wonder of the scene was upon them.

Presently Maida, finding a stone conveniently placed, sat down on the sand and used the stone for a back. Lenox threw himself at her feet. From the downs above there came now and then the slumberous tinkle of a bell, but so faintly that it fused with the rustle of the waves; no one heard it save a little girl who was tending cattle and who knew by the tinkle where each of her charges browsed. She was a ragged child, barefooted and not very wise; she was afraid of strangers with the vague fear that children have. And at times during the summer, when tourists crossed the downs where her cattle were, she would hide till they had passed.

On this afternoon she had been occupying herself with blades of grass, which she threw in the air and watched float down to the shore below, but at last she had wearied of this amusement and was about to turn and bully the cows in the shrill little voice which was hers, when Maida and her companion appeared on the scene. The child felt almost secure; nothing but a bird could reach her from the shore and of birds she had no fear, and so, being curious and not very much afraid, she watched the couple with timid, inquisitive eyes.

For a long time she watched and for a long time they remained motionless in the positions which they had first chosen. At times the sound of their voices reached her. She wished she were a little nearer that she might hear what they said. She had never seen people sit on the beach before, though she had heard that people sometimes did so, all night, too, and that they were called smugglers. But somehow the people beneath her did not seem to belong to that category. For a moment she thought that they might be guarding the coast, and at that thought an inherent instinctive fear of officials beat in her small breast. She had indeed heard of female smugglers; there was her own aunt, for instance; but no, she had never heard of a coast-guard in woman's clothes. That idea had to be dismissed, and so she wondered and watched until she forgot all about them, and turned her attention to a white sail in the open.

The white sail fainted in sheets of cobalt. The sun which had neared the horizon was dying in throes of crimson and gamboge. It was time she knew to drive the cattle home. She stood up and brushed her hair aside, and as she did so, her eyes fell again on the couple below. The man had moved; he was not lying as he had been with his back to the bluff; he was kneeling by his companion, her head was on his shoulder, her arms were about his neck, and his mouth was close to hers. The little maid smiled knowingly; she had seen others in much the same attitude; the mystery was dissolved; they were neither guards nor smugglers—they were lovers; and she ran on at once through the bramble and called shrilly to the cows.

The excursionists, meanwhile, had reached Hendaye and had been ferried across the stream that flows between it and Fuenterrabia. At the landing they were met by a gentleman in green and red who muttered some inquiry. The boatman undid the straps of the valise which they bore, and this rite accomplished, the gentleman in green and red looked idly in them and turned as idly away. The boatman shouldered the valises again, and started for the inn.

Mr. Incoul and his friend were both men to whom the visible world exists and they followed with lingering surprise. They ascended a sudden slope, bordered on one side by a high white wall in which lizards played, and which they assumed was the wall of some monastery, but which they learned from the boatman concealed a gambling-house, and soon entered a small grass-grown plaza. To the right was a church, immense, austere; to the left were some mildewed dwellings; from an upper window a man with a crimson turban looked down with indifferent eyes and abruptly a bird sang.

From the plaza they entered the main street and soon were at the inn. Mr. Incoul and Blydenburg were both men to whom the visible world exists, but they were also men to whom the material world has much significance. In the hall of the inn a chicken and two turkeys clucked with fearless composure. The public room was small, close and full of insects. At a rickety table an old man, puffy and scornful, was quarreling with himself on the subject of a *peseta* which he held in his hand. The inn-keeper, a frowsy female, emerged from some remoter den, eyed them with unmollifiable suspicion and disappeared.

"We can't stop here," said Blydenburg with the air of a man denying the feasibility of a trip to the moon.

On inquiry they learned that the town contained nothing better. At the Casino there were roulette tables, but no beds. Travelers usually stopped at Hendaye or at Irun.

"Then we will go back to Biarritz."

They sent their valises on again to the landing place and then set out in search of Objects of Interest. The palace of Charlemagne scowled at them in a tottering, impotent way. When they attempted to enter the church, a chill caught them neck and crop and forced them back. For some time they wandered about in an aimless, unguided fashion, yet whatever direction they chose that direction fed them firmly back to the landing place. At last they entered the Casino.

The grounds were charming, a trifle unkempt perhaps, the walks were not free from weeds, but the air was as heavy with the odor of flowers as a perfumery shop in Bond street. In one alley, in a bower of trees, was a row of tables; the covers were white and the glassware unexceptionable.

"We could dine here," Blydenburg said in a self-examining way. A pretty girl of the manola type, dressed like a soubrette in a vaudeville, approached and decorated his lapel with a tube-rose. "We certainly can dine here," he repeated.

The girl seemed to divine the meaning of his words. "*Ciertamente, Caballero*," she lisped.

Mr. Blydenburg had never been called *Caballero* before, and he liked it. "What do you say, Incoul?" he asked.

"I am willing, order it now if you care to."

But the ordering was not easy. Mr. Blydenburg had never studied pantomime, and his gestures were more indicative of a patient describing a toothache to a dentist than of an American citizen ordering an evening meal. "*Kayry-Oostay*," he repeated, and then from some abyss of memory he called to his aid detached phrases in German.

The girl laughed blithely. Her mouth was like a pomegranate cut in twain. She took a thin book bound in morocco from the table and handed it to the unhappy gentleman. It was, he found, a list of dishes and of wines. In his excitement, he pointed one after another to three different soups, and then waving the book at the girl as who should say, "I leave the rest to you," he dared Mr. Incoul to go into the Casino and break the bank for an appetizer.

The Casino, a low building of leprous white, stood in the centre of the garden. At the door, a lackey, in frayed, ill-fitting livery, took their sticks and gave them numbered checks in exchange. The gambling-room was on the floor above, and occupied the entire length of the house. There, about a roulette table, a dozen men were seated playing in a cheap and vicious way for small stakes. They looked exactly what they were, and nothing worse can be said of them. "A den of thieves in a miniature paradise," thought Mr. Blydenburg, and his fancy was so pleased with the phrase that he determined to write a letter to the *Evening Post*, in which, with that for title, he would give a description of Fuenterrabia. He found a seat and began to play. Mr. Incoul looked on for a moment and then sought the reading-room. When he returned Blydenburg had a heap of counters before him.

"I have won all that!" he exclaimed exultingly. He looked at his watch, it was after seven. He cashed the counters and together they went down again to the garden.

The dinner was ready. They had one soup, not three, and other dishes of which no particular mention is necessary. But therewith was a bottle of Val de Peñas, a wine so delicious that a temperance lecturer suffering from hydrophobia would have drunk of it. The manola with the pomegranate mouth fluttered near them, and toward the close of the meal Mr. Blydenburg chucked her under the chin. "Nice girl that," he announced complacently.

"I dare say," his friend answered, "but I have never been able to take an interest in women of that class."

Blydenburg was flushed with winnings and wine. He did not notice the snub and proceeded to relate an after-dinner story of that kind in which men of a certain age are said to luxuriate. Mr. Incoul listened negligently.

"God knows," he said at last, "I am not a Puritan, but I like refinement, and refinement and immorality are incompatible."

"Fiddlesticks! Look at London, look at Paris, New York even; there are women whom you and I both know, women in the very best society, of whom all manner of things are said and known. You may call them immoral if you want to, but you cannot say that they are not refined."

"I say this, were I related in any way, were I the brother, father, the husband of such a woman, I would wring her neck. I believe in purity in women, and I believe also in purity in men."

"Yes, it's a good thing to believe in, but it's hard to find."

Mr. Incoul had spoken more vehemently than was his wont, and to this remark he made no answer. His eyes were green, not the green of the cat but the green of a tiger, and as he sat with fingers clinched, and a cheerless smile on his thin lips, he looked a modern hunter of the Holy Grail.

The night train leaves Hendaye a trifle after ten, and soon a *sereno* was heard calling the hour, and declaring that all was well. It was time to be going, they knew, and without further delay they had themselves ferried again across the stream. The return journey was unmarked by adventure or incident. Mr. Blydenburg fell into a doze, and after dreaming of the pomegranate mouth awoke at Biarritz, annoyed that he had not thought to address the manola in Basque. At the station they found a carriage, and, as Blydenburg entered it, he made with himself a little consolatory pact that some day he would go back to Fuenterrabia alone.

The station at Biarritz is several miles from the town, and as the horses were slow it was almost twelve o'clock before the Continental was reached. Blydenburg alighted there and Mr. Incoul drove on alone to the villa. As he approached it he saw that his wife's rooms were illuminated. For the moment he thought she might be waiting for him, but at once he knew that was impossible, for on leaving he had said he would pass the night in Spain.

The carriage drew up before the main entrance. He felt for small money to pay the driver, but found nothing smaller than a louis. The driver, after a protracted fumbling, declared that in the matter of change he was not a bit better of. Where is the cabman who was ever supplied? Rather than waste words Mr. Incoul gave him the louis and the man drove off, delighted to find that the old trick was still in working order.

Mr. Incoul looked up again at his wife's window, but during his parley with the driver the lights had been extinguished. He entered the gate and opened the door with a key. The hall was dark; he found a match and lit it. On the stair was Lenox Leigh. The match flickered and went out, but through the open door the moon poured in.

The young man rubbed his hat as though uncertain what to do or say. At last he reached the door, "I am at the Grand, you know," he hazarded.

"Yes, I know," Mr. Incoul answered, "and I hope you are comfortable."

Leigh passed out. Mr. Incoul closed and bolted the door behind him. For a moment he stood very still. Then turning, he ascended the stair.

CHAPTER X.
THE POINT OF VIEW.

On leaving the villa Lenox Leigh experienced a number of conflicting emotions, and at last found relief in sleep. The day that followed he passed in chambered solitude; it was possible that some delegate from Mr. Incoul might wish to exchange a word with him, and in accordance with the unwritten statutes of what is seemly, it behooved him to be in readiness for the exchange of that word. Moreover, he was expectant of a line from Maida, some word indicative of the course of conduct which he should pursue, some message, in fact, which would aid him to rise from the uncertainty in which he groped. As a consequence he remained in his room. He was not one to whom solitude is irksome, indeed he had often found it grateful in its refreshment, but to be enjoyable solitude should not be coupled with suspense; in that case it is uneasiness magnified by the infinite. And if fear be analyzed, what is it save the dread of the unknown? When the nerves are unstrung a calamity is often a tonic. The worst that can be has been done, the blow has fallen, and with the falling fear vanishes, hope returns, the healing process begins at once.

The uneasiness which visited Lenox Leigh came precisely from his inability to determine whether or not a blow was impending. As to the blow, he cared, in the abstract, very little. If it were to be given, let it be dealt and be done with; that which alone troubled him was his ignorance of what had ensued after his meeting with Mr. Incoul, and his incapacity to foresee in what manner the consequences of that meeting would affect his relations with Mr. Incoul's wife.

In this uncertainty he looked at the matter from every side, and, that he might get the broadest view, he recalled the incidents connected with the meeting. The facts of the case seemed then to resolve themselves into this: Mr. Incoul had unexpectedly returned to his home after midnight, and had met a friend of his wife's descending the stair. Their greeting, if formal, had been perfectly courteous. The departing guest had informed the returning husband at what hotel he was stopping, and that gentleman had expressed the hope that he was comfortable. Certainly there was nothing extraordinary in that. People who dwelled in recondite regions might see impropriety in a call that extended up to and beyond midnight, whereas others who lived in more liberal centres might consider it the most natural thing in the world. It was, then, merely the point of view, and what was the point of view which Mr. Incoul had adopted? If he considered it an impropriety why had he seemed so indifferent? And, if he considered it natural and proper, why should he have been so damned civil? Why should he have expressed the hope that his wife's guest was comfortable at a hotel? Was the expression of that hope merely a commonplace rejoinder, or was it an intentional slur? Surely, every one possessed of the brain of a medium-sized rabbit feels that it is as absurd to expect an intelligent being to be comfortable in a hotel as it is to suppose that he can find enjoyment in an evening party or amusement in a comic paper. Then again, and this, after all, was the great question: was the return of Mr. Incoul intentional or accidental? If it was intentional, if he had gone away intending that he would be absent all night merely that by an unexpected return he might verify any suspicions which he may have harbored, then in driving to his door in a rumbling coach he had shown himself a very poor plotter. On the other hand, if the return were accidental had it served to turn a suspicionless husband into a suspicious one, and if it had so served, how far did those suspicions extend? Did he think that his wife and her guest had been occupied with aimless chit-chat, or did he believe that their conversation had been of a personal and intimate nature?

As Lenox pondered over these things it seemed to him that, let Mr. Incoul suspect what he might, the one and unique cause for apprehension lay in the attitude which Maida had assumed when her husband, after closing the door, had gone to her in search of an explanation. That he had so gone there was to him no possible doubt. And it was in the expectancy of tidings as to the result of that explanation that he waited the entire day in his room.

But the afternoon waned into dusk and still no tidings came. As the hours wore on his uneasiness decreased. "Bah!" he muttered to himself at last, "in the winter I gave all my mornings to Pyrrho and Ænesidemus, and here six months later during an entire day I bother myself about eventualities."

He sighed wearily with an air of self-disgust, and rising from the sofa on which his meditations had been passed he went to the window. The Casino opposite was already illuminated. "They will be there to-night," he thought. "I have been a fool for my pains. If Maida hasn't written it is because there has been nothing to write. I will look them up after dinner and everything will be as before." He took off his morning suit and got himself into evening dress. He tied his white cravat without emotion, with a precision that was geometric in its accuracy, and to hold the tie in place he ran a silver pin through the collar without so much as pricking his neck. He was thoroughly at ease. The fear of the blow had passed. Pyrrho, Ænesidemus, the whole corps of ataraxists had surged suddenly and rescued him from the toils of the inscrutable.

At a florist's in the street below he found an orchid with which he decked his button-hole, and then in search of dinner he sauntered into Helder's, a restaurant on the main street, a trifle above the Grand Hôtel. It was crowded; there did not seem to be a single table unoccupied. He hesitated for a moment, and was about to go elsewhere when he noticed some one signaling to him from the remoter end of the garden. He could not at first make out who it was and it was not until he had made use of a monocle that he recognized a fellow Baltimorean, Mr. Clarence May, with whom in days gone by he had been on terms approaching those of intimacy.

Mr. Clarence May, more familiarly known as Clara, was a pigeon-shooter who for some years past had been promenading the side scenes of continental life. He was well known in the penal colonies of the Riviera, and hand-in-glove with some of the most distinguished *rastaquouères*, yet did he happen in a proscenium it was by accident. In appearance he was not beautiful: he was a meagre little man, possessed of vague features and an allowance of sandy hair so undetermined that few were able to remember whether or not he wore any on his face. When he spoke it was with a slight stutter, a trick of speech which he declared he had inherited from his wet-nurse.

He rose from his seat, and hurrying forward, greeted Lenox as though he had seen him the week before. He was anything but an idealist, yet he treated Time as though it were the veriest fiction of the non-existent, and he bombarded no one with questions as to what had become of them, or where had they been.

"I have just ordered dinner," he said, in his amusing stammer, "you must share it with me." And Lenox, who had not a prejudice to his name, accepted the invitation as readily as it was made.

"I don't know," May continued, when they were seated—"I don't know whether you will like the dinner—I have ordered very little. No soup, too hot, don't you think? No oysters, there are none; all out visiting, the man said; for fish I have substituted a melon; fish, at the seaside, is never good; then we are to have white truffles, with a plain sauce, a chateaubriand, salad, a bit of cheese—*voilà!* How will that suit you?"

Lenox nodded, as who should say, had I ordered it myself it could not be more to my taste, and thus encouraged, May offered him a glass of Amer Picon, a beverage that smells like an orange and looks like ink.

The dinner passed off pleasantly enough. The white truffles were excellent, and the chateaubriand cooked to a turn. The only fault to be found was with the Brie, which May seemed to think was not as flowing as it should be.

"By the way," he said at last when coffee was served, "you know Mirette is here?"

"Mirette? Who is Mirette?"

"Why, good gad! My dear fellow, Mirette is Mirette; the one adorable, unique, divine Mirette. You don't mean to say you never heard of her!"

"I do, though perhaps she may have had the good fortune to hear of me."

"Heavens alive, man! don't you read the papers?"

Lenox smiled. "Why should I? I am not interested in the community. It might be stricken with dry-rot, elephantiasis and plica polonica for ought I care. Besides, there is nothing in them; the English papers are all advertisements and aridity, the French are frivolous and obscene. I mind neither frivolity nor obscenity; both have their uses, as flowers and cesspools have theirs; but I object to them served with my breakfast. I think if once a year a man would read a summary of the twelvemonth, he would get in ten minutes a digest of all that might be necessary to know, and what is more to the point, he would have to his credit a clear profit of two hundred hours at the very least, and two hundred hours rightly employed are sufficient for the acquirement of such a knowledge of a foreign language as will permit a man to make love in it gracefully. No, I seldom read the papers, so forgive my ignorance as to Mirette."

"After such an explanation I shall have to. But if you care to learn by word of mouth that which you decline to read in print, Mirette is *premier sujet.*"

"In the ballet, you mean."

"Yes, in the ballet, and I can't for the life of me think of a ballet without her."

"She must have gone to your head."

"And to every one's who has seen her."

"You say she is here?"

"Yes, she'll be at the Casino to-night; I'll present you if you say so."

"I might take a look at her, but I fancy I shalt be occupied elsewhere."

"As you like." May drew out his watch. "It's after nine," he added, "if we are going to the Casino we had better be t-toddling."

On the way there May entered a tobacconist's, and Lenox waited for him without. As he loitered on the curb, Blydenburg rounded an adjacent corner.

"Well," exclaimed the latter, "you didn't see our friends off."

"What friends?"

"The Incouls of course; didn't you know that they had gone?"

Lenox looked at him blankly. "Gone," he echoed.

"Yes, they must have sent you word. Incoul seemed to expect you. They have gone up to Paris. If I had known beforehand—"

Mr. Blydenburg rambled on, but Lenox no longer listened. It was for this then that he had been bothering himself the entire day. The abruptness of the departure mystified him, yet he comforted himself with the thought that had there been anything abnormal, it could not have escaped Blydenburg's attention.

"And you say they expected me?" he asked at last.

"Yes, they seemed to. Incoul left good-bye for you. When you get to Paris look them up."

While he was speaking May came out from the tobacconist's.

"I will do so," Lenox said, and with a parting nod he joined his friend.

As he walked on down the road to the Casino, Mr. Blydenburg looked musingly after him. He would not be a bad match for Milly, he told himself, not a bad match at all; and thinking that perhaps it might be but a question of bringing the two young people together, he presently started off in search of his daughter and led her, lamb-like, to the Casino. But once there he felt instinctively that for that evening at least any bringing together of the young people was impossible. Lenox was engaged in an animated conversation with a conspicuously dressed lady, whom, Mr. Blydenburg learned on inquiry, was none other than the notorious Mlle. Mirette, of the Théâtre National de l'Opéra.

CHAPTER XI.
THE HOUSE IN THE PARC MONCEAU.

There had been a crash in Wall street. Two of the best houses had gone under. Of one of these the senior partner had had recourse to the bare bodkin. For several years previous his wife had dispensed large hospitality from a charming hôtel just within the gates of the Parc Monceau. At the news of her ruined widowhood she fled from Paris. In a week it was only her creditors that remembered her. The hôtel was sold under the hammer. A speculator bought it and while waiting a chance to sell it again at a premium, offered it for rent, fully furnished, as it stood. This by the way.

After the dinner in Spain, Mr. Incoul passed some time in thought. The next morning he sent for Karl, and after a consultation with him, he went to the square that overhangs the sea, entered the telegraph office, found a blank, wrote a brief message, and after attending to its despatch, returned to the villa. His wife was in the library, and as he entered the room the *maître d'hôtel* announced that their excellencies were served.

Maida had never been more bewildering in her beauty. Her lips were moist, and under her polar-blue eyes were the faintest of semicircles.

"Did you enjoy your trip to Fuenterrabia?" she asked.

"Exceedingly," he answered. But he did not enter into details and the breakfast was done before either of them spoke again.

At last as Maida rose from the table Mr. Incoul said: "We leave for Paris at five this afternoon. I beg you will see to it that your things are ready."

She steadied herself against a chair, she would have spoken, but he had risen also and left the room.

For the time being her mind refused to act. Into the fibres of her there settled that chill which the garb and aspect of a policeman produces on the conscience of a misdemeanant. But the chill passed as policemen do, and a fever came in its place.

To hypnotize her thoughts she caught up an English journal. She read of a cocoa that was grateful and comforting, the praises of Pear's Soap, an invitation from Mr. Streeter to view his wares, a column of testimonials on the merits of a new pill, appeals from societies for pecuniary aid. She learned that a Doré was on exhibition in New Bond street, that Lady Grenville, The Oaks, Market Litchfield, was anxious to secure a situation for a most excellent under-housemaid, that money in large amounts or small could be obtained without publicity on simple note of hand by applying personally or by letter to Moss & Lewes, Golden Square. She found that a harmless, effective and permanent cure for corpulency would be sent to any part of the world, post-paid, on receipt twelve stamps, and that the Junior Macready Club would admit a few more members without entrance fee. She read it all determinedly, by sheer effort of will, and at last in glancing over an oasis her eye fell upon a telegram from Madrid which stated cholera had broken out afresh.

She took the paper with her and hurried from the room. In the hall her husband stood talking to Karl. She went to him and pointed to the telegram. "Is it for this we are to leave?" she asked.

He read the notice and returned it. "Yes," he answered, "it is for that." And then it was that both chill and fever passed away.

The journey from Biarritz was accomplished without incident. On their previous visit to Paris, they had put up at the Bristol and to that hostelry they returned. The manager had been notified and the yellow suite overlooking the Palace Vendôme was prepared for their reception. On arriving, Maida went at once with her maid to her room. Mr. Incoul changed his clothes, passed an hour at the Hamman, breakfasted at Voisin's, and then had himself driven to a house-agent.

The clerk, a man of fat and greasy presence, gave him a list of apartments, marking with a star those which he thought might prove most suitable. Mr. Incoul visited them all. He had never lived in an apartment in Paris and the absence of certain conveniences perplexed him. The last apartment of those that were starred was near the Arc de Triomphe. When he had been shown it over he found a seat, and heedless of the volubility of the concierge, rested his head in his hand and thought. For the moment it seemed to him as though it would be best to return to New York, but there were objections to that, and reflecting that there might be other and better arranged apartments, he left the chattering concierge and drove again to the agent's.

"I have seen nothing I liked," he said simply.

At this the clerk expressed his intense surprise. The apartment in the Avenue Montaigne was everything that there was of most fine, and wait, the Hospodar of Wallachia had just quitted the one in the Rue de Presbourg. "It astonishes me much," he said.

The astonishment of the clerk was to Mr. Incoul a matter of perfect indifference. "Have you any private houses?" he asked.

"Ah, yes, particular hôtels." Yes, there was one near the Trocadero, but for his part he found that the apartment in the Avenue Montaigne would fit him much better. "But now that I am there," he continued, "I recall myself of one that is enchanter as a subjunctive. I engage you to visit it." And thereupon he wrote down the address of the house in the Parc Monceau.

It was not, Mr. Incoul discovered, a large dwelling, but the appointments left little to be desired. In the dressing-rooms was running water, and each of the bed-rooms was supplied with gas-fixtures. He touched one to see if it were in working order, and immediately the escaping ether assured him that it was. He sniffed it with a feeling akin to pleasure. One would have thought that since he left Madison avenue he had not enjoyed such a treat. There was gas to be found in the dining-room, but the reception-rooms were furnished with lamps and candelabras. The bed-rooms were on the floor above. One of these overlooked the park. There was a dressing-room next to it, but to the two rooms there was but one entrance, and that from the hall. This little suite, Mr. Incoul resolved, should be occupied by his wife. Beyond, across the hall, was a sitting-room, and at the other end of the house was a second suite, which Mr. Incoul mentally selected for himself.

He returned to the agent, and informed him that the house suited him, an announcement which the man received with an air of personal sympathy.

"Is it not!" he exclaimed, "it made the mouth champagne nothing but to think there. And again, one was at home with one's self. Truly, the hôtel was beautiful as a boulevard. Monsieur would never regret himself of it. And had Monsieur servants? No, good then. Let Monsieur not disquiet himself. He who spoke knew of a cook, veritably a blue ribbon, and as to masters of hôtel, why, anointed name of a dog, not later than yesterday, he had heard that Baptiste—he who had served the family of Cantacuzène—Monsieur knew her, without doubt, came to be free."

In many respects Paris is not what it might be. The shops are vulgar in their ostentation. Were Monte Cristo to return he would find his splendor cheap and commonplace. In a city where Asiatic magnificence is sold from misfit and remnant counters by the ton, where emeralds large as swallows' eggs are to be had in the side-streets at a discount, where agents are ready to provide everything from an opéra-seria to a shoelace, the *badauds* have lost their ability to be startled. Paris, moreover, is not what it was. The suavity and civility for which it was proverbial have gone the way of other old-fashioned virtues; the wit which used to run about the streets never by any chance enters a salon; save in China a more rapacious set of bandits than the restauranteurs and shop-keepers do not exist; the theatres are haunts of ennui; the boulevards are filled with the worst-dressed set of people in the world. As for Parisian gaiety, there is nothing duller—no, not even a carnival. In winter the city is a tomb; in summer a furnace. In fact, there are dozens and dozens of places far more attractive, but there is not one where house-keeping is easier. The butcher and baker are invisible providers of the best of fare. The servants understand their duties and attend to them, and, given a little forethought and a good bank account, the palace of the White Cat is there the most realizable of constructions.

In a week's time the house in the Parc Monceau ran in grooves. To keep it running the tenants had absolutely nothing to do but to pay the bills. For this function Mr. Incoul was amply prepared, and, that the establishment should be on a proper footing, he furnished an adjacent stable with carriages, grooms and horse.

CHAPTER XII.
MR. INCOUL IS PREOCCUPIED.

Mr. Incoul's attitude to his wife had, meanwhile, in no wise altered. To an observer, nay, to Maida herself, he was as silent, methodical and self-abnegatory as he had been from the first. He had indeed caused her to send a regret to Ballister without giving any reason why the regret should be sent, but otherwise he showed himself very indulgent.

He cared little for the stage, yet to gratify Maida he engaged boxes for the season at the Français and at the Opéra. Now and then in the early autumn when summer was still in the air he took her to dine in the Bois, at Madrid or Armenenville, and drove home with her in the cool of the evening, stopping, perhaps, for a moment at some one of the different concerts that lined the Champs Elysées. And sometimes he went with her to Versailles and at others to Vincennes, and one Sunday to Bougival. But there Maida would never return; it was crowded with a set of people the like of which she had never seen before, with women whose voices were high pitched and unmodulated, and men in queer coats who stared at her and smiled if they caught her eye.

But with the first tingle that accompanies the falling leaves, the open-air restaurants and concerts closed their doors. There was a succession of new plays which Vitu always praised and Sarcey always damned. The verdict of the latter gentleman, however, did not affect Maida in the least. She went bravely to the Odéon and liked it, to the Cluny where she saw a shocking play that made her laugh till she cried. She went to the Nations and saw Lacressonière and shuddered before the art of that wonderful actor. At the Gymnase she saw the "Maître des Forges" and when she went home her eyes were wet; she saw "Nitouche" and would have willingly gone back the next night to see it again; even Mr. Incoul smiled; nothing more irresistibly amusing than Baron could be imagined; she saw, too, Bartet and Delaunay, and for the first time heard French well spoken. But of all entertainments the Opéra pleasured her most. Already, under Mapleson's reign, she had wearied of mere sweetness in music; she felt that she would enjoy Wagner and even planned a pilgrimage to Bayreuth, but meanwhile Meyerbeer had the power to intoxicate her very soul. The septette in the second act of "L'Africaine" affected her as had never anything before; it vibrated from her fingertips to the back of her neck; the entire score, from the opening notes of the overture to the farewell of Zuleika's that fuses with the murmur of the sea, thrilled her with abrupt surprises, with series and excesses of delight.

There were, of course, many evenings when neither opera nor theatre was attractive, and on such evenings invitations from resident friends and acquaintances were sometimes accepted and sometimes open house was held.

On these occasions, Maida found herself an envied bride. It was not merely that her husband was rich enough to buy a principality and hand it over for charitable purposes, it was not merely that he was willing to give her everything that feminine heart could desire, it was that, however crowded the halls might be, he seemed conscious of the existence of but one woman, and that woman was his wife. There were triflers who said that this attitude was *bourgeois*; there were others—more witty—who said that it was immoral; but, be this as it may, the South American highwaymen, who called themselves generals, the Russian princesses, the Roumanian boyards, the attachés, embassadors, and other accredited bores, the contingent from the Faubourg, the American residents, who, were they sent in a body to the rack, could not have confessed to an original thought among them, all these, together with a sprinkling of Spaniards and English, the Tout-Paris, in fact, agreed, as it was intended they should, on this one point, to wit, that Mr. Incoul was the most devoted of husbands.

And such apparently he was. If Maida had any lingering doubts as to the real reason of their return to Paris, little by little they faded. After her fright she made with herself several little compacts, and that she might carry them out the better she wrote to Lenox a short, decisive note. She determined that he should never enter her life again. It was no longer his, he had let it go without an effort to detain it, and in Biarritz if it had seemed that he still held the key of her heart, it was owing as much to the unexpectedness of his presence as to the languors of the afternoons. In marrying, she had meant to be brave; indeed, she had been so—when there was no danger; and if in spite of her intentions she had faltered, the faltering had at least served as a lesson which she would never need to learn again. Over the cinders of her youth she would write a Requiescat. Her girlhood had been her own to give, but her womanhood she had pledged to another.

As she thought of these things she wondered at her husband. He had done what she had hardly dared to expect—he had observed their ante-nuptial agreement to the letter. A brother could not have treated her with greater respect. Surely if ever a man set out to win his wife's affection he had chosen the surest way. And why had he so acted if it were not as he had said, that given time and opportunity he *would* win her affection. He was doing so, Maida felt, and with infinitely greater speed than she had ever deemed possible. Beside, if the mangled remnants of her heart seemed attractive, why should he be debarred from their possession? Yet, that was precisely the point; he did not know of the mangled remnants, he thought her heart-whole and virginal. But what would he do if he learned the truth? And as she wondered, suddenly the consciousness came to her that she was living with a stranger.

Heretofore she had not puzzled over the possible intricacies of her husband's inner nature. She had known that he was of a grave and silent disposition, and as such she had been content to accept him, without question or query. But as she collected some of the scattered threads and memories of their life in common, it seemed to her that latterly he had become even graver and more silent than before. And this merely when they were alone. In the presence of a third person, when they went abroad as guests, or when they remained at home as hosts, he put his gravity aside like a garment. He encouraged her in whatever conversation she might have engaged in, he aided her with a word or a suggestion, he made a point of consulting her openly, and smiled approvingly at any bright remark she chanced to make.

But when they were alone, unless she personally addressed him, he seldom spoke, and the answers that he gave her, while perfectly courteous in tone and couching, struck her, now that she reflected, as automatic, like phrases learned by rote. It is true they were rarely alone. In the mornings he busied himself with his correspondence, and in the afternoons she found herself fully occupied with shops and visits, while in the evenings there was usually a dinner, a play, or a reception, sometimes all three. Since the season had begun, it was only now and then, once in ten days perhaps, that an evening was passed *en tête-à-tête.* On such occasions he would take up a book and read persistently, or he would smoke, flicking the ashes from the cigar abstractedly with his little finger, and so sit motionless for hours, his eyes fixed on the cornice.

It was this silence that puzzled her. It was evident that he was thinking of something, but of what? It could not be archæology, he seemed to have given it up, and he was not a metaphysician, the only thinker, be it said, to whom silence is at all times permissible.

At first she feared that his preoccupation might in some way be connected with the episodes at Biarritz, but this fear faded. Mr. Incoul had been made a member of the Cercle des Capucines, and now and then looked in there ostensibly to glance at the papers or to take a hand at whist. One day he said casually, "I saw your friend Leigh at the club. You might ask him to dinner." The invitation was sent, but Lenox had regretted. After that incident it was impossible for her to suppose that her husband's preoccupation was in anywise connected with the intimacy which had subsisted between the young man and herself.

There seemed left to her then but one tenable supposition. Her husband had been indulgence personified. He had been courteous, refined and foreseeing, in fact a gentleman, and, if silent, was it not possible that the silence was due to a self-restraining delicacy, to a feeling that did he speak he would plead, and that, perhaps, when pleading would be distasteful to her?

To this solution Maida inclined. It was indeed the only one at which she could arrive, and, moreover, it conveyed that little bouquet of flattery which has been found grateful by many far less young and feminine than she. And so, one evening, for the further elucidation of the enigma, and with the idea that perhaps it needed but a word from her to cause her husband to say something of that which was on his mind, and which she was at once longing and dreading to hear—one evening when he had seemed particularly abstracted, she bent forward and said, "Harmon, of what are you thinking?"

She had never called him by his given name before. He started, and half turned.

"Of you," he answered.

But Maida's heart sank. She saw that his eyes were not in hers, that they looked over and beyond her, as though they followed the fringes of an escaping dream.

CHAPTER XIII.
WHAT MAY BE HEARD IN A GREENROOM.

One evening in November a new ballet was given at the Opéra. Its production had been heralded in the manner which has found most favor with Parisian impressarii. The dead walls of the capital were not adorned with colored lithographs. The advertising sheets held no notice of the coming performance. But for several weeks previous the columns of the liveliest journals had teemed with items and discreet indiscretions.

Through these measures the curiosity of the Tout-Paris had been coerced afresh, and, when the curtain, after falling on the second act of the "Favorite" parted again before the new ballet, there was hardly a vacant seat in the house.

The box which Mr. Incoul had taken for the season was on what is known as the grand tier. It was roomy, holding eight comfortably and twelve if need be. But Maida, who was adverse to anything that suggested crowding, was always disinclined to ask more than five or six to share it with her, and on the particular evening to which allusion is made she extended her hospitality to but four people: Mr. and Mrs. Wainwaring and their daughter, New Yorkers like herself, and the Duc de la Dèche, a nobleman who served as figure-head to the Cercle des Capucines, and who, so ran the gossip, was anxious to effect an exchange of his coroneted freedom for the possession of Miss Wainwaring and a bundle or two of her father's securities.

During the *entr'acte* that preceded the ballet the box was invaded by a number of visitors, young men who were indebted to Maida for a dinner or a cup of tea and by others who hoped that such indebtedness was still in store for them; there came, too, a popular artist who wished to paint Maida's portrait for the coming Salon and an author who may have had much cleverness, but who never displayed it to any one.

As the invasion threatened to continue Mr. Incoul went out in the corridor, where he was presently joined by the duke, who suggested that they should visit the foyer. They made their way down the giant stair and turning through the lobby passed on through the corridor that circles the stalls until they reached a door guarded from non-subscribers by a Suisse about whose neck there drooped a medallioned chain of silver. By him the door was opened wide and the two men passed on through a forest of side scenes till the *foyer de la danse* was reached.

It was a spacious apartment, well lighted and lined with mirrors; the furniture was meagre, a dozen or more chairs and lounges of red plush. It was not beautiful, but then what market ever is? To Mr. Incoul it was brilliant as a café, and equally vulgar. From dressing-rooms above and beyond there came a stream of willowy girls. Few among them were pretty, and some there were whose faces were repulsive, but the majority were young; some indeed, the rats, as they are called, were mere children. Here and there was a mother of the Mme. Cardinal type, armed with an umbrella and prepared to listen to offers. As a rule, however, the young ladies of the ballet were quite able to attend to any little matter of business without maternal assistance. The Italian element was easily distinguishable. There was the ultra darkness of the eye, the faint umber of the skin, the richer vitality, in fact, of which the anemic daughters of Paris were unpossessed. And now and then the Gothic gutturals of the Spanish were heard, preceded by a wave of garlic.

That night the subscribers to the stalls were out in full force. There were Jew bankers in plenty, there were detachments from the Jockey and the Mirletons, one or two foreign representatives, a few high functionaries, the Minister of the Interior, and he of the Fine Arts, a member of the imperial family of Russia, a number of stock brokers and an Arab Sheik flanked by an interpreter.

Before the curtain rose, battalions of ballerines formed on the stage, and after the performance began they were succeeded by others, the first contingent returning to the dressing-rooms or loitering in the foyer. In this way there was a constant coming and going accompanied by the murmur of the spectators beyond and the upper notes of the flute.

Mr. Incoul was growing weary; he would have returned to the box, but he was joined by acquaintances that he had made at the club, Frenchmen mainly, friends of his companion, and presently he found himself surrounded by a group of *viveurs*, men about town, who had their Paris at the end of their gloves, and to whom it held no secrets. They had dined and talked animatedly in ends and remnants of phrases in a sort of verbal telegraphy; an exclamation helped by a gesture sufficing as often as not for the full conveyance of their thought.

Mr. Incoul spoke French with tolerable ease, but having nothing of moment to say, he held his tongue, contenting himself with listening to the words of those who stood about him. And as he listened, the name of Mirette caught his ear. The programme had already informed him that it was she who was to assume the principal rôle in the new ballet, consequently he was not unfamiliar with it, but of the woman herself he knew nothing, and he listened idly, indifferent to ampler information. But at once his interest quickened; his immediate neighbor had mentioned her in connection with one whom he knew.

"They came up from Biarritz together," he heard him say. "She went there with Chose, that Russian."

"Balaguine?"

"Precisely."

"What did she do with him?"

"Found the Tartar, I fancy."

"And then?"

"*Voilà*, this young American is mad about her."

"He is rich then?"

"What would you? An American! They are it all."

"Yes, a rich one always wins."

"How mean you?"

"This: he plays bac at the Capucines. His banks are fructuous."

"Ah, as to that—" And the first speaker shrugged his shoulders.

A rustle circled through the foyer, men stood aside and nodded affably. The lights took on a fairer glow. "Stay," murmured the second speaker, "she is there."

Through the parting crowd Mirette passed with a carriage such as no queen, save perhaps Semiramis, ever possessed. She moved from the hips, her body was erect and unswayed. It was the perfection of artificial grace. Her features were not regular, but there was an expression in them that stirred the pulse. "*Je suis l'Amour*," she seemed to say, and to add "*prends garde à toi*." As she crossed the room men moistened their lips, and when she had gone they found them still parched.

Mr. Incoul followed her with his eyes. She had not left him unimpressed, but his impression differed from that of his neighbors. In her face his shrewdness had discerned nothing but the animal and the greed of unsatiated appetites. He watched her pass, and stepped from the group in which he had been standing that he might the better follow her movements.

From the foyer she floated on into a side scene, yet not near enough to the stage to be seen by the audience. A few machinists moved aside to let her pass, and as they did so Mr. Incoul saw Lenox Leigh. It was evident that he had been waiting there for her coming. There was a scarf about her neck, and as the young man turned to greet her, she took it off and gave it into his keeping. They whispered together. Beyond, Mr. Incoul could see the tulle of the ballet rising and subsiding to the rhythm of the orchestra. Then came a sudden blare of trumpets, the measure swooned, and as it recovered again the ballet had faded to the back of the stage. Abruptly, as though sprung from a trap-door, a *régisseur* appeared, and at a signal from him Mirette, with one quick backward stroke to her skirt, bounded from the side scene and fluttered down to the footlights amid a crash and thunder of applause.

Mr. Incoul had heard and seen enough. His mind was busy. He felt the need of fresh air and of solitude. He turned into the corridor and from there went through the vestibule until he reached an outer door, which he swung open and passed out into the night. He was thinly clad, in evening dress, and the air was chilly, but he thought nothing of his dress nor of the warmth or chill of the air. He walked up and down before the building with his head bent and his hands behind his back. A *camelot* offered him a pack of transparent cards, a vender of programmes pestered him to buy, but he passed them unheeding. For fully half an hour he continued his walk, and when he re-entered the box, Maida, who of late had given much attention to his moods, noticed that his face was flushed, and that about his lips there played the phantom of a smile.

CHAPTER XIV.
KARL GROWS A MOUSTACHE.

For several days Mr. Incoul was much occupied. He left the house early and returned to it late. One afternoon he sent for Karl. Since the return to Paris the courier's duties had not been arduous; they consisted chiefly in keeping out of the way. On this particular afternoon he was not immediately discoverable, and when at last he presented himself it was in the expectation that the hour of his dismissal had struck. He bowed, nevertheless, with the best grace in the world, and noticing that his employer's eyes were upon him, gazed deferentially at the carpet.

Mr. Incoul looked at him in a contemplative way for a moment or two. "Karl," he said at last, and Karl raised his eyes.

"Yes, sir."

"Have you any objections to shaving your whiskers?"

"I, sir? not the slightest."

"I will be obliged if you will do so. This afternoon you might go to Cumberland's and be measured. I have left orders there. Then take a room at the Meurice; you have money, have you not? Very good, keep an account of your expenditures. In a week I will send you my instructions. That will do for to-day."

An hour later Mr. Incoul was watching a game of baccarat at the Cercle des Capucines.

Meanwhile Lenox Leigh had given much of his time to the pleasures of Mirette's society. In making her acquaintance at Biarritz he had been actuated partly by the idleness of the moment and partly by the attracting face of celebrity. He had never known a danseuse; indeed, heretofore, his acquaintance with women had been limited to those of his own *monde*, and during the succeeding days he hovered about her more that he might add a new photograph to a mental album than with any idea of conquest. She amused him extremely. In her speech she displayed a recklessness of adjective such as he had never witnessed before. It was not that she was brilliant, but she possessed that stereotyped form of repartee which is known as *bagou*, and which the Parisian takes to naturally and without effort. Mirette seemed to have acquired it in its supremest expression. One day, for instance, the curiosity of her circle of admirers was aroused by a young actress who, while painfully plain, squandered coin with remarkable ease. "Whom do you suppose she gets the money from?" some one asked, and Mirette without so much as drawing breath answered serenely, "A blind man." In spite of the *bagou* Mirette was not a Parisian. She was born in the provinces, at Orléans, and was wont to declare herself a lineal descendant of Joan of Arc. She lied with perfect composure; if reproached she curled her lips. "Lies whiten the teeth," she would say, an argument which it was impossible to refute.

Under the empire she would have been a success; under a republic she complained of the difficulty of making two ends meet. Now Lenox was not rich, but he was an American, and the Americans have assumed in Paris the position which the English once held. Their coffers are considered inexhaustible. On this subject, thanks to Mrs. Mackay, Mr. Incoul, the Vanderbilts, the Astors and a dozen others, there is now no doubt in the mind of the French. To be an American is to be a Vesuvius of gold pieces.

As a native of the land of millions, Lenox found that his earliest attentions were received with smiles, and in time when a Russian became so scratched that the Tartar was visible, Mirette welcomed him with undisguised favor.

Like many another, Lenox had his small vanities; he would have liked to have thought himself indispensable to Maida's happiness, but in her absence he did not object to being regarded as the *cavaliere servente* of the first lady of the ballet. Between the two women the contrast was striking. Mirette, as has been hinted, was reckless of adjective; she was animal, imperious, and at times frankly vulgar. Maida was her antithesis. She shrank from coarseness as from a deformity. Both represented Love, but they represented the extremes. One was as ignorant of virtue as the other was unconscious of vice. One was Mylitta, the other Psyche. Had the difference been less accentuated, it would have jarred. But the transition was immeasurable. It was like a journey from the fjords of Norway to the jungles of Hindustan. That Psyche was regretted goes without the need of telling, but Mylitta has enchantments which are said to lull regret.

In the second week of October the bathing was still delicious. The waves encircled one in a large, abrupt embrace. Mirette would have liked to remain, the beach was a daily triumph for her. There was not a woman in the world who could have held herself in the scantiest of costumes, under the fire of a thousand eyes, as gracefully as she. No sedan-chair for her indeed. No hurrying, no running, no enveloping wrap. No pretense or attempt to avoid the scrutiny of the bystanders. There was nothing of this for her. She crossed the entire width of sand, calmly, slowly, an invitation on her lips and with the walk and majesty of a queen. The amateurs as usual were tempted to applaud. It was indeed a triumph, an advertisement to boot, and one which she would have liked to prolong. But she was needed at the Opéra and so she returned to Paris accompanied by Lenox Leigh.

In Paris it is considered inconvenient for a pretty woman to go about on foot, and as for cabs, where is the self-respecting chorus-girl who would consent to be seen in one? Mirette was very positive on this point and Lenox agreed with her thoroughly. He did not, however, for that reason offer to provide an equipage. Indeed the wherewithal was lacking. He had spent more money at Biarritz than he had intended, perhaps ten times the amount that he would have spent at Newport or at Cowes, and his funds were nearly exhausted.

As every one is aware a banker is the last person in the world to be consulted on matters of finance. If a client has money in his pocket a banker can transfer it to his own in an absolutely painless manner, but if the client's pocket is empty what banker, out of an opéra-bouffe, was ever willing to fill it? Lenox reflected over this and was at a loss how to act. The firm on whom his drafts were drawn held nothing on their ledgers to his credit. He visited them immediately on arriving and was given a letter which for the moment he fancied might contain a remittance. But it bore the Paris postmark and the address was in Maida's familiar hand. As he looked at it he forgot his indigence, his heart gave an exultant throb. He had promised himself that when he met her again matters should go on very much as they had before, and he had further promised himself that so soon as his former footing was re-established he would give up Mirette. He was therefore well pleased when the note was placed in his hands. It had a faint odor of orris, and he opened it as were he unfolding a lace handkerchief. But from what has gone before it will be understood that his pleasure was short lived. The note was brief and categoric, he read it almost at a glance, and when he had possessed himself of the contents he felt that the determination conveyed was one from which there was no appeal, or rather one from which any appeal would be useless. He looked at the note again. The handwriting suggested an unaccustomed strength, and in the straight, firm strokes he read the irrevocable. "It is done," he muttered. "I can write Finis over that." He looked again at the note and then tore it slowly into minute scraps, and watched them flutter from him.

He went out to the street and there his earlier preoccupation returned. It would be a month at least before a draft could be sent, and meanwhile, though he had enough for his personal needs, he had nothing with which to satisfy Mirette's caprices. *Et elle en avait, cette dame!* The thought of separating from her did not occur to him, or if it did it was in that hazy indistinguishable form in which eventualities sometimes visit the perplexed. If Maida's note had been other, he would have washed his hands of Mirette, but now apparently she was the one person on the Continent who cared when he came and when he went. In his present position he was like one who, having sprained an ankle, learns the utility of a crutch. The idea of losing it was not agreeable. Beside, the knowledge that his intimacy with the woman had been envied by grandees with unnumbered hats was to him a source of something that resembled consolation.

Presently he reached the boulevard. He was undecided what to do or where to turn, and as he loitered on the curb the silver head of a stick was waved at him from a passing cab; in a moment the vehicle stopped. May alighted and shook him by the hand.

"I am on my way to the Capucines," he explained, in his blithesome stutter. "There's a big game on; why not come, too?"

"A big game of what?"

"B-b, why baccarat of course. What did you suppose? M-marbles?"

Lenox fumbled in his waistcoat pocket. "Yes, I'll go," he said.

Five minutes later he was standing in a crowded room before a green table. He had never gambled, and hardly knew one card from another, but baccarat can be learned with such facility that after two deals a raw recruit can argue with a veteran as to whether it is better to stand on five or to draw. Lenox watched the flight of notes, gold and counters. He listened to the monotonous calls: *J'en donne! Carte! Neuf!* The end of the table at which he stood seemed to be unlucky. He moved to the other, and presently he leaned over the shoulder of a gamester and put down a few louis. In an hour he left the room with twenty-seven thousand francs.

A fraction of it he put in his card-case, the rest he handed to Mirette. It was not a large sum, but its dimensions were satisfactory to her. "*Ce p'tit chat*," she said to herself, "*je savais bien qu'il ne ferait pas le lapin.*" And of the large azure notes she made precisely one bite.

Thereafter for some weeks things went on smoothly enough. Mirette's mornings were passed at rehearsals, but usually the afternoons were free, and late in the day she would take Lenox to the Cascade, or meet him there and drive back with him to dinner. In the evenings there was the inevitable theatre, with supper afterwards at some *cabaret à la mode*. And sometimes when she was over-fatigued, Lenox would go to the club and try a hand at baccarat.

He was not always so fortunate as on the first day, but on the whole his good luck was noticeable. It is possible, however, that he found the excitement enervating. He had been used to a much quieter existence, one that if not entirely praiseworthy was still outwardly decorous, and suddenly he had been pitch-forked into that narrowest of circles which is called Parisian life. He may have liked it at first, as one is apt to like any novelty, but to nerves that are properly attuned a little of its viciousness goes a very great way.

It may be that it was beginning to exert its usual dissolvent effect. In any event Lenox, who all his life had preferred water to wine, found absinthe grateful in the morning.

One afternoon, shortly after the initial performance of the new ballet, he went from his hotel to the apartment which Mirette occupied in the Rue Pierre-Charon. He was informed that she was not at home. He questioned the servant as to her whereabouts, but the answers he received were vague and unsatisfactory. He then drove to the Cascade, but Mirette did not appear. After dinner he made sure of finding her. In this expectation he was again disappointed.

The next day his success was no better. He questioned the servant uselessly. "Madame was not at home, she had left no word." To each of his questions the answer was invariable. It was evident that the servant had been coached, and it was equally evident that at least for the moment his companionship was not a prime necessity to the first lady of the ballet.

As he left the house he bit his lip. That Mirette should be capricious was quite in the order of things, but that she should treat him like the first comer was a different matter. When he had last seen her, her manner had left nothing to be desired, and suddenly, without so much as a p. p. c., her door was shut, and not shut as it might have been by accident; no, it was persistently, purposely closed.

Presently he reached the Champs-Elysées. It was Sunday. A stream of carriages flooded the avenue, and the sidewalks were thronged with ill-dressed people. The crowd increased his annoyance. The possibility of being jostled irritated him, the spectacle of dawdling shop-keepers filled him with disgust. He hailed a cab in which to escape; the driver paid no attention; he hailed another; the result was the same, and then in the increasing exasperation of the moment he felt that he hated Paris. A fat man with pursed lips and an air of imbecile self-satisfaction brushed against him. He could have turned and slapped him in the face.

Without, however, committing any overt act of violence, he succeeded in reaching his hotel. There he sought the reading-room, but he found it fully occupied by one middle-aged Englishwoman, and leaving her in undisturbed possession of the *Times*, he went to his own apartment. A day or two before he had purchased a copy of a much applauded novel, and from it he endeavored to extract a sedative. Mechanically he turned the pages. His eyes glanced over and down them, resting at times through fractions of an hour on a single line, but the words conveyed no message to his mind, his thoughts were elsewhere, they surged through vague perplexities and hovered over shadowy enigmas, until at last he discovered that he was trying to read in the dark.

He struck a light and found that it was nearly seven. "I will dress," he told himself, "and dine at the club." In half an hour he was on his way to the Capucines. The streets were still crowded and the Avenue de l'Opéra in which his hotel was situated, vibrated as were it the main artery of the capital. As he approached the boulevard he thought that it would perhaps be wiser to dine at a restaurant; he was discomfited and he was not sure but that the myriad tongue of gossip might not be already busy with the cause of his discomfiture. He did not feel talkative, and were he taciturn at the club he knew that it would be remarked. Bignon's was close at hand. Why not dine there? In his indecision he halted before an adjacent shop and stood for a moment looking in the window, apparently engrossed by an assortment of strass and imitation pearls. The proprietress was lounging in the doorway. "*Si Monsieur veut entrer*"—she began seductively, but he turned from her; as he did so, a brougham drew up before the curb and Mirette stepped from it.

Lenox, in his surprise at the unexpected, did not at first notice that a man had also alighted. He moved forward and would have spoken, but Mirette looked him straight in the eyes, as who should say *Allez vous faire lanlaire, mon cher*, and passed on into the restaurant.

Her companion had hurried a little in advance to open the door, and as he swung it aside and Mirette entered Lenox caught a glimpse of his face. It was meaningless enough, and yet not entirely unfamiliar. "Who is the cad," he wondered. Yet, after all, what difference did it make? He could not blame the man. As for jealousy, the word was meaningless to him. It was his *amour propre* that suffered. He smiled a trifle grimly to himself and continued his way.

At the corner was a large picture shop. An old man wrapped in a loose fur coat stood at the window looking at the painting of a little girl. The child was alone in a coppice and seemingly much frightened at the approach of a flock of does. Unconsciously Lenox stopped also. He had been so bewildered by the suddenness of the cut that he did not notice whether he was walking or standing still.

And so it was for this, he mused, that admittance had been denied him. But why could she not have had the decency to tell him not to come instead of letting him run there like a tradesman with a small bill? Certainly he had deserved better things of her than that. It was so easy for a woman to break gracefully. A note, a word, and if the man insists a second note, a second word; after that the man, if he is decently bred, can do nothing but raise his hat and speed the parting guest. Beside, why would she want to break with him and take up with a fellow who looked like a barber from the Grand Hôtel? Who was he any way?

His eyes rested on the picture of the little girl. The representation of her childish fright almost diverted his thoughts, but all the while there was an undercurrent which in some dim way kept telling him that he had seen the man's face before. And as he groped in his memory the picture of the child faded as might a picture in a magic lantern, and in its place, vaguely at first and gradually better defined, he saw, standing in the moonlight, on a white road, a coach and four. To the rear was the terrace of a hôtel, and beyond was a shimmering bay like to that which he had seen at San Sebastian.

"My God," he cried aloud, "it's Incoul's courier!"

The old man in the fur coat looked at him nervously, and shrank away.

CHAPTER XV.
MAY EXPOSTULATES.

That evening the Wainwarings and the Blydenburgs dined at the house in the Parc Monceau. The Blydenburgs had long since deserted Biarritz, but the return journey had been broken at Luchon, and in that resort the days had passed them by like chapters in a stupid fairy tale.

They were now on their way home; the pleasures of the Continent had begun to pall, and during the dinner, Mr. Blydenburg took occasion to express his opinion on the superiority of American institutions over those of all other lands, an opinion to which he lent additional weight by repeating from time to time that New York was quite good enough for him.

There were no other guests. Shortly before ten the Wainwarings left, and as Blydenburg was preparing to take his daughter back to the hotel, Mr. Incoul said that he would be on the boulevard later, and did he care to have him he would take him to the club, a proposition to which Blydenburg at once agreed.

"Harmon," said Maida, when they were alone, "are you to be away long?"

During dinner she had said but little. Latterly she had complained of sleeplessness, and to banish the insomnia a physician had recommended the usual bromide of potassium. As she spoke, Mr. Incoul noticed that she was pale.

"Possibly not," he answered.

She had been standing before the hearth, her bare arm resting on the velvet of the mantel, and her eyes following the flicker of the burning logs—but now she turned to him.

"Do you remember our pact?" she asked.

He looked at her but said nothing. She moved across the room to where he stood; one hand just touched his sleeve, the other she raised to his shoulder and rested it there for a second's space. Her eyes sought his own, her head was thrown back a little, from her hair came the perfume of distant oases, her lips were moist and her neck was like a jasmine.

"Harmon," she continued in a tone as low as were she speaking to herself, "we have come into our own."

And then the caress passed from his sleeve, her hand fell from his shoulder, she glided from him with the motion of a swan.

"Come to me when you return," she added. Her face had lost its pallor, it was flushed, but her voice was brave.

Yet soon, when the door closed behind him, her courage faltered. In the eyes of him whose name she bore and to whom for the first time she had made offer of her love, she had seen no answering affection—merely a look which a man might give who wins a long-contested game of chess. But presently she reassured herself. If at the avowal her husband had seemed triumphant, in very truth what was he else? She turned to a mirror that separated the windows and gazed at her own reflection. Perhaps he did think the winning a triumph. Many another would have thought so, too. She was entirely in white; her arms and neck were unjeweled. "I look like a bride," she told herself, and then, with the helplessness of regret, she remembered that brides wear orange blossoms, but she had none.

The idler in Paris is apt to find Sunday evenings dull. There are many houses open, it is true, but not infrequently the idler is disinclined to receptions, and as to the theatres, it is *bourgeois* to visit them. There is, therefore, little left save the clubs, and on this particular Sunday evening, when Mr. Incoul and Blydenburg entered the Capucines, they found it tolerably filled.

A lackey in silk knee breeches and livery of pale blue came to take their coats. It was not, however, until Blydenburg had been helped off with his that he noticed that Mr. Incoul had preferred to keep his own on.

The two men then passed out of the vestibule into a room in which was a large table littered with papers, and from there into another room where a man whom Mr. Incoul recognized as De la Dèche was dozing on a lounge, and finally a room was reached in which most of the members had assembled.

"It reminds me of a hotel," said Blydenburg.

"It is," his friend answered shortly. He seemed preoccupied as were he looking for some one or something; and presently, as they approached a green table about which a crowd was grouped, Blydenburg pulled him by the sleeve.

"That's young Leigh dealing," he exclaimed.

To this Mr. Incoul made no reply. He put his hand in a lower outside pocket of his overcoat and assured himself that a little package which he had placed there had not become disarranged.

On hearing his name, Lenox looked up from his task. A Frenchman who had just entered the room nodded affably to him and asked if he were lucky that evening.

"Lucky!" cried some one who had caught the question, "I should say so. His luck is something insolent; he struck a match a moment ago and *it lit*."

The whole room roared. French matches are like French cigars in this, there is nothing viler. It is just possible that the parental republic has views of its own as to the injuriousness of smoking, and seeks to discourage it as it would a vice. But this is as it may be. Every one laughed and Lenox with the others. Mr. Incoul caught his eye and bowed to him across the table. Blydenburg had already smiled and bowed in the friendliest way. He did not quite care to see Mrs. Manhattan's brother dealing at baccarat, but after all, when one is at Rome—

"Do you care to play?" Mr. Incoul asked.

"Humph! I might go a louis or two for a flyer."

They had both been standing behind the croupier, but Mr. Incoul then left his companion, and passing around the table stopped at a chair which was directly on Lenox's left. In this chair a man was seated, and before him was a small pile of gold. As the cards were dealt the gold diminished, and when it dwindled utterly and at last disappeared, the man rose from his seat and Mr. Incoul dropped in it.

From the overcoat pocket, in which he had previously felt, he drew out a number of thousand-franc notes; they were all unfolded, and under them was a little package. The notes, with the package beneath them, were placed by Mr. Incoul where the pile of gold had stood. One of the notes he then threw out in the semicircle. A man seated next to him received the cards which Lenox dealt.

"I give," Lenox called in French.

"Card," the man answered.

It was a face card that he received.

"Six," Lenox announced.

Mr. Incoul's neighbor could boast of nothing. The next cards that were dealt on that end of the table went to a man beyond. Mr. Incoul knew that did that man not hold higher cards than the banker the cards in the succeeding deal would come to him.

He took a handful of notes and reached them awkwardly enough across the space from which Lenox dealt; for one second his hand rested on the talion, then he said, "*À cheval.*" Which, being interpreted, means half on one side and half on the other. The croupier took the notes, and placed them in the proper position. "Nine," Lenox called; he had won at both ends of the table.

The croupier drew in the stakes with his rake. "Gentlemen," he droned, "make your game."

Mr. Incoul pushed out five thousand francs. The next cards on the left were dealt to him.

"Nine," Lenox called again.

And then a very singular thing happened. The croupier leaned forward to draw in Mr. Incoul's money, but just as the rake touched the notes, Mr. Incoul drew them away.

"*Monsieur!*" exclaimed the croupier.

The eyes of every one were upon him. He pushed his chair back, and stood up, holding in his hand the two cards which had been dealt him, then throwing them down on the table, he said very quietly, but in a voice that was perfectly distinct, "These cards are marked."

A moment before the silence had indeed been great, but during the moment that followed Mr. Incoul's announcement, it was so intensified that it could be felt. Then abruptly words leapt from the mouths of the players and bystanders. The croupier turned, protesting his innocence of any complicity. There may have been some who listened, but if there were any such, they were few; the entire room was sonorous with loud voices; the hubbub was so great that it woke De la Dèche; he came in at one door rubbing his eyes; at another a crowd of lackeys, startled at the uproar, had suddenly assembled. And by the chair which he had pushed from him and which had fallen backwards to the ground, Mr. Incoul stood, motionless, looking down at Lenox Leigh.

In the abruptness of the accusation Lenox had not immediately understood that it was directed against him, but when he looked into the inimical faces that fronted and surrounded him, when he heard the anger of the voices, when he saw hands stretched for the cards which he dealt, and impatient eyes examining their texture, and when at last, though the entire scene was compassed in the fraction of a minute, when he heard an epithet and saw that he was regarded as a Greek, he knew that the worst that could be had been done.

He turned, still sitting, and looked his accuser in the face, and in it he read a message which to all of those present was to him alone intelligible. He bowed his head. In a vision like to that which is said to visit the last moments of a drowning man, he saw it all: the reason of Maida's unexplained departure, the coupling of Mirette with a servant, and this supreme reproach made credible by the commonest of tricks, the application of a cataplasm, a new deck of cards on those already in use. It was vengeance indeed.

He sprang from his seat. He was a handsome fellow and the pallor of his face made his dark hair seem darker and his dark eyes more brilliant. "It is a plot," he cried. He might as well have asked alms of statues. The cards had been examined, the *maquillage* was evident. "Put him out!" a hundred voices were shouting; "*à la porte!*"

Suddenly the shouting subsided and ceased. Lenox craned his neck to discover who his possible defender might be, and caught a glimpse of De la Dèche, brushing with one finger some ashes from his coat sleeve, and looking about him with an indolent, deprecatory air.

"Gentlemen," he heard him say, "the committee will act in the matter; meanwhile, for the honor of the club, I beg you will not increase the scandal."

He turned to Lenox and said, with perfect courtesy, "Sir, do me the favor to step this way."

Through the parting crowd Lenox followed the duke. In crossing the room he looked about him. On his way he passed the Frenchman who had addressed him five minutes before. The man turned aside. He passed other acquaintances. They all seemed suddenly smitten by the disease known as *Noli me tangere*. In the doorway was May. Of him he felt almost sure, but the brute drew back. "Really," he said, "I must exp-postulate."

"Expostulate and be damned," Lenox gnashed at him. "I am as innocent as you are."

In an outer room, where he presently found himself, De La Dèche stood lighting a cigar; that difficult operation terminated, he said, slowly, with that rise and fall of the voice which is peculiar to the Parisian when he wishes to appear impressive:

"You had better go now, and if you will permit me to offer you a bit of advice, I would recommend you to send a resignation to any clubs of which you may happen to be a member."

He touched a bell; a lackey appeared.

"Maxime, get this gentleman's coat and see him to the door."

CHAPTER XVI.
THE BARE BODKIN.

Presently Lenox found himself on the boulevard. There was a café near at hand, and he sat down at one of the tables that lined the sidewalk. He was dazed as were he in the semi-consciousness of somnambulism. He gave an order absently, and when some drink was placed before him, he took it at a gulp.

Under its influence his stupor fell from him. The necessity, the obligation of proving his innocence presented itself, but, with it, hand in hand, came the knowledge that such proof was impossible. Even his luck at play would be taken as corroboratory of the charge. Were he to say that the marked cards had been placed on the talion by Incoul, who was there outside the aisles of the insane that would listen to such a defense? To compel attention, he would be obliged to explain the act, and state its reason. And that explanation he could never give. He could not exculpate himself at the cost of a woman's fame. Which ever way he turned, dishonor stood before him. The toils into which he had fallen had been woven with a cunning so devilish in its clairvoyance that every avenue of escape was closed. He was blockaded in his own disgrace.

He rested his head in his hand, and moaned aloud. Presently, with the instinct of a hunted beast, he felt that people were looking at him. He feared that some of his former acquaintances, on leaving the club, had passed and seen him sitting there, and among them, perhaps Incoul.

He threw some money in the saucer and hurried away. There were still many people about. To avoid them he turned into a side street and walked on with rapid step. Soon he was in the Rue de la Paix. It was practically deserted. On a corner, a young ruffian in a slouch hat was humming, "*Ugène, tu m'fais languir,*" and beating time to the measure with his foot. Just above the Colonne Vendôme the moon rested like a vagrant, weary of its amble across the sky. But otherwise the street was solitary. Through its entire length but one shop was open, and as Lenox approached it a man came out to arrange the shutters. From the doorway a thin stream of light still filtered on the pavement. In the window were globes filled with colored liquids, and beyond at a counter a clerk was tying a parcel.

Lenox entered. "Give me a Privas," he said, and when the clerk had done so, he asked him to make up a certain prescription. But to this the man objected; he could not, he explained, without a physician's order.

"Here are several," said Lenox, and he took from his card-case a roll of azure notes.

The clerk eyed them nervously. They represented over a year's salary. He hesitated a moment, "I don't know,"—and he shook his head, as were he arguing with himself—"I don't know whether I am doing right." And at once prepared the mixture.

Ten minutes later Lenox was mounting the stair of the hotel at which he lodged. On reaching his room he put his purchases on a table, poured out a glass of absinthe, lit a cigarette, and threw himself down on a lounge. For a while his thoughts roamed among the episodes of the day, but gradually they drifted into less personal currents. He began to think of the early legends: of Chiron, the god, renouncing his immortality; of the Hyperboreans, that fabled people, famous for their felicity, who voluntarily threw themselves into the sea; of Juno bringing death to Biton and Cleobis as the highest recompense of their piety; of Agamedes and Trophonius, praying Apollo for whatever gift he deemed most advantageous, and in answer to the prayer receiving eternal sleep.

He reflected on the meaning of these legends, and, as he reflected, he remembered that the Thracians greeted birth with lamentations and death with welcoming festivals. He thought of that sage who pitied the gods because their lives were unending, and of Menander singing the early demise of the favored. He remembered how Plato had preached to the happiest people in the world the blessedness of ceaseless sleep; how the Buddha, teaching that life was but a right to suffer, had found for the recalcitrant no greater menace than that of an existence renewed through kalpas of time. Then he bethought him of the promise of that peace which passeth all understanding, and which the grave alone fulfills, and he repeated to himself Christ's significant threat, "In this life ye shall have tribulation."

And, as these things came to him, so, too, did the problem of pain. He reviewed the ravages of that ulcer which has battened on humanity since the world began. History uncoiled itself before him in a shudder. In its spasms he saw the myriads that have fought and died for dogmas that they did not understand, for invented principles of patriotism and religion, for leaders that they had never seen, for gods more helpless than themselves.

He saw, too, Nature's cruelty and her snares. The gift to man of appetites, which, in the guise of pleasure, veil immedicable pain. Poison in the richest flowers, the agony that lurks in the grape. He knew that whoso ate to his hunger, or drank to his thirst, summoned to him one or more of countless maladies—maladies which parents gave with their vices to their children, who, in turn, bring forth new generations that are smitten with all the ills to which flesh is heir. And he knew that even those who lived most temperately were defenceless from disorders that come unawares and frighten away one's nearest friends. While for those who escaped miasmas and microbes; for those who asked pleasure, not of the flesh, but of the mind; for those whose days are passed in study, who seek to learn some rhyme for the reason of things, who try to gratify the curiosity which Nature has given them; for such as they, he remembered, there is blindness, paralysis, and the asylums of the insane.

He thought of the illusions, of love, hope and ambition, illusions which make life seem a pleasant thing worth living, and which, in cheating man into a continuance of his right to suffer, make him think pain an accident and not the rule.

"Surely," he mused, "the idiot alone is content. He at least has no illusions; he expects nothing in this world and cares less for another. Nor is the stupidity of the ordinary run of men without its charm. It must be a singularly blessed thing not to be sensitive, not to know what life might be, and not to find its insufficiency a curse. But there's the rub. When the reforms of the utopists are one and all accomplished, what shall man do in his Icaria? A million years hence, perhaps, physical pain will have been vanquished. Diseases of the body will no longer exist. Laws will not oppress. Justice will be inherent. Love will be too far from Nature to know of shame. The earth will be a garden of pleasure. Industry will have enriched every home. Through an equitable division of treasures acquired without toil, each one will be on the same footing as his neighbor. Even envy will have disappeared. In place of the trials, terrors and superstitions of to-day, man will enjoy perfect peace. He will no longer labor. When he journeys it will be through the air. He will be in daily communication with Mars, he will have measured the Infinite and know the bounds of Space. And in this Eden in which there will be no forbidden fruit, no ignorance, no tempter, but where there will be larger flowers, new perfumes, and a race whose idea of beauty stands to mine as mine does to that of prehistoric man, a race whose imagination has crossed the frontiers of the impossible, who have developed new senses, who see colors to which I am blind, who hear music to which I am deaf, who speak in words of tormented polish, who have turned art into a plaything and learning into a birthright, a race that has no curiosity and who accept their wonderful existence as the rich to-day accept their wealth, in this Eden, Boredom will be King. The Hyperboreans will have their imitators. The one surcease will be in death. Yet even that may not be robbed of its grotesqueness."

A candle flickered a moment and expired in a splutter of grease. The agony of the candle aroused him from his revery. "Bah," he muttered, "I am becoming a casuist, I argue with myself."

He mixed himself another absinthe, holding the *carafe* high in the air, watching the thin stream of water coalesce with the green drug and turn with it into an opalescent milk. He toyed for a moment with the purchases that he had made in the Rue de la Paix, and presently, in answer to some query which they evoked, the soliloquy began anew.

"After what has happened there is nothing left. I might change my name. I might go to Brazil or Australia, but with what object? I could not get away from myself.

Da me stesso
Sempre fuggendo, avrò me sempre appresso.

Beside I don't care for transplantation. If I had an ambition it would be a different matter. If I could be a pretty woman up to thirty, a cardinal up to fifty, and after that the Anti-Christ, it might be worth while. Failing that I might occupy myself with literature. If I have not written heretofore, it is because it seems more original not to do so. But it is not too late. The manufacture of trash is easy, and it must be a pleasure to the manufacturer to know that it is trash and that it sells. It must give him a high opinion of the intellect of his contemporaries. Or when, as happens now and then, a work of enduring value is produced, and it is condemned, as such works usually are, the author must take immense delight in the reflection that the disapproval of imbeciles is the surest acknowledgement of talent, as it is also its sweetest mead of praise. For me, of course, such praise is impossible. Were I to write successful failures, it must needs be under a pseudonym. In which case I would have the consciousness of being scorned as Lenox Leigh, and admired as John Smith. Beside, what is there to write about? There is nothing to prove, there is no certainty, there is not even a criterion of truth. To-morrow contradicts yesterday, next week will contradict this. On no given subject are there two people who think and see exactly alike. The book which pleases me bores my neighbor, and *vice versâ*. One man holds to the Episcopal Church, another to the Baptist; one man is an atheist, another a Jew; one man thinks a soprano voice a delicious gift, another says it is a disease of the larynx, and whatever the divergence of opinion may be, each one is convinced that he alone is correct. Supposing, however, that through some chance I were to descend to posterity in the garb and aspect of a great man. What is a great man? The shadow of nothing. The obscurest *privat docent* in Germany could to-day give points to Newton. And even though Newton's glory may still subsist, yet such are the limitations of fame that the great majority have never heard of it or of him. The foremost conqueror of modern times, he who fell not through his defeats, but through his victories, is entombed just across the Seine. And the other day as I passed the Invalides

I heard an intelligent-looking woman ask her companion who the Napoleon was that lay buried there. Her companion did not know.

"But, even were glory more substantial, what is the applause of posterity to the ears of the dead? To them honor and ignominy must be alike unmeaning. No, decidedly, ambition does not tempt me. And what is there else that tempts? Love seems to me now like hunger, an unnecessary affliction, productive far more of pain than of pleasure; the most natural, the most alluring thing of all, see in what plight it has brought me. Yet it is, I have heard, the ultimate hope of those who have none. If I relinquish it, what have I left? The satisfaction of my curiosity as to what the years may hold? But I am indifferent. To revenge myself on Incoul. Certainly, I would like to cut his heart out and force it down his throat! But how would it better me? If I could be transported to the multicolored nights of other worlds, and there taste of inexperienced pleasures, move in new refinements, lose my own identity, or pursue a chimera and catch it, it might be worth while, but, as it is—"

The clock on the mantel rang out four times. Again Lenox started from his revery. He smiled cynically at himself. "If I continue in that strain," he muttered, "it must be that I am drunk."

But soon his eyes closed again in mental retrospect. "And yet," he mused, "life is pleasant; ill spent as mine has been, many times I have found it grateful. In books, I have often lost the consciousness of my own identity; now and then music has indeed had the power to take me to other worlds, to show me fresh horizons and larger life. Maida herself came to me like a revelation. She gave me a new conception of beauty. Yes, I have known very many pleasant hours. I was younger then, I fancy. After all, it is not life that is short, it is youth. When that goes, as mine seems to have done, outside of solitude there is little charm in anything. And what is death but isolation? The most perfect and impenetrable that Nature has devised. And whether that isolation come to me to-night or decades hence, what matters it? It is odd, though, how the thought of it unnerves one, and yet, to be logical, I suppose one should be as uneasy of the chaos which precedes existence as of the unknowable that follows it. The proper course, I take it, is to imitate the infant, who faces death without a tremor, and enters it without regret."

He stood up, and drawing the curtains aside, looked out into the night. From below came the rumble of a cart on its way to the Halles, but otherwise the street was silent. The houses opposite were livid. There was a faint flicker from the street lamps, and above were the trembling stars. The moon had gone, but there was yet no sign of coming dawn.

He left the window. The candles had burned down; he found fresh ones and lighted them. As he did so, he caught sight of himself in the glass. His eyes were haggard and rimmed with circles. It was owing to the position of the candles, he thought, and he raised them above his head and looked again. There was something on his forehead just above the temple, and he put the candles down to brush that something away. He looked again, it was still there. He peered into the glass and touched it with his hand. It was nothing, he found, merely a lock of hair that had turned from black to white.

He poured out more absinthe, and put the bottle down empty. Before drinking it he undid the package which he had bought from the chemist. First he took from it a box about three inches long. In it was a toy syringe, and with it two little instruments. One of these he adjusted in the projecting tube, and with his finger felt carefully of the point. It was sharp as a needle, and beneath the point was an orifice like a shark's mouth, in miniature.

Then he took from the package a phial that held a brown liquid, in which he detected a shade like to that of gold. The odor was dull and heavy. He put the phial down and stood for a moment irresolute. He had looked into the past and now he looked into the future. But in its Arcadias he saw nothing, save his own image suspended from a gibbet. He looked again almost wistfully; no, there was nothing. He threw off his coat and rolled up his sleeve. From the phial he filled the syringe, and with the point pricked the bare arm and sent the liquid spurting into the flesh. Three times he did this. He reached for the absinthe and left it untasted.

Into his veins had come an unknown, a delicious languor. He sank into a chair. The walls of the room dissolved into cataracts of light and dazzling steel. The flooring changed to running crimson, and from that to black, and back to red again. From the ceiling came flood after flood of fused, intermingled and oscillating colors. His eyes closed. The light became more intense, and burned luminous through the lids. In his ears filtered a harmony, faint as did it come from afar, and singular as were it won from some new consonance of citherns and clavichords, and suddenly it rose into tumultuous vibrations, striated with series of ascending scales. Then as suddenly ceased, drowned in claps of thunder.

The lights turned purple and glowed less vividly, as though veils were being lowered between him and them. But still the languor continued, sweeter ever and more enveloping, till from very sweetness it was almost pain.

The room grew darker, the colors waned, the lights behind the falling veils sank dim, and dimmer, fading, one by one; a single spark lingered, it wavered a moment, and vanished into night.

CHAPTER XVII.
MAIDA'S NUPTIALS.

For some time after Lenox had gone there was much excitement at the Capucines. But gradually the excitement wore itself out, as excitement always does. Baccarat for that night, at least, had lost its allurement. The habitués dispersed, some to other clubs, some to their homes, and soon the great rooms were deserted by all, save one deaf man, who, undisturbed by the commotion, had given himself up to the task of memorizing Sarcey's feuilleton.

Among the earliest to leave was Mr. Incoul. "Come," he said to Blydenburg, "you have seen enough for one evening," and Blydenburg got into his coat and followed his companion to the street. They walked some distance before either of them spoke, but when they reached the hotel at which Blydenburg was stopping, that gentleman halted at an adjacent lamp-post.

"I must say, Incoul," he began, "and I hope you will take it very kindly—I must say that I think you might have left that matter for some one else to discover. Why, hang it all! Leigh is a friend of your wife's; you know all his people; to you the money was nothing. Really, Incoul, damn me if I don't think it hard-hearted. I don't care that for what those frog-eaters say; the cards you said were marked, don't weigh with me in the least; no, not an atom; it is my opinion that the young man was just as innocent as a child unborn. No, sir, you can't make me believe that he—that he—I hate to say the word—that he cheated. Why, man alive! I had my eyes on him the whole time. A better-looking fellow never breathed, and he just chucked out the cards one after another without so much as looking at them; it seemed to me that he didn't care a rap whether he won or lost. I put down a louis or two myself, and he never noticed it; he left the whole thing to the croupier, and now that I come to think of it—"

"Yes, I know," Mr. Incoul interrupted. "I am sorry myself."

"Well then I'll be shot if you look so. Good night to you," and with that Blydenburg stamped up to the hotel, rang the bell, and slammed the door behind him.

Mr. Incoul walked on. The annoyance of his friend affected him like a tonic; he continued his way refreshed. Presently he reached a cab stand. The clock marked 11.50. He had other duties, and he let himself into an Urbaine and told the man to drive to the Parc Monceau. On arriving he tossed a coin to the cabby and entered the house.

In the vestibule a footman started from a nap. Mr. Incoul went up to the floor above and waited, the door ajar. For a little space he heard the man moving about, whispering to a fellow footman. But soon the whispering ceased. Evidently the men had gone. Assured of this, he opened a drawer and took from it a steel instrument, one that in certain respects resembled a key; the haft, however, was unusually large, the end was not blunt but hollow, yet fashioned like a pincer, and the projecting tongue which, in the case of an ordinary key serves to lock and unlock, was absent. This he put in his pocket. He went out in the hall and listened again. The house was very quiet. He made sure that the footmen had really gone, and walking on tip-toe to his wife's door, rapped ever so noiselessly.

"Is it you, Harmon?" he heard her ask. Had he wished he had no time to answer. A key turned in the lock, the door was opened, and before him Maida stood, smiling a silent welcome to his first visit to her room.

As he entered and closed the door her lips parted; she would have spoken, but something in his face repelled her; the smile fell from her face and the words remained unuttered.

He stood a moment rubbing his hands frigidly, as were he cold, yet the room was not chilly. There was no fire in the grate, but two gas fixtures gave out sufficient heat to warm it unassisted. Then presently he looked at her. She had thrown herself on a lounge near the hearth, and was certainly most fair to see. Her white gown had been replaced by one of looser cut; her neck and arms were no longer bare, but one foot shod in fur that the folds of the skirt left visible was stockingless and the wonder of her hair was unconfined.

He found a chair and seated himself before her. "Madam," he said at last, "I am here at your request."

The girl started as were she stung.

"You were obliging enough this evening to inform me that we had come into our own. What is it?" His eyebrows were raised and about his thin lips was just the faintest expression of contempt. "What is it into which we have come?"

Maida grew whiter than the whitest ermine; she moved her hand as would she answer, but he motioned her to be silent.

"I will tell you," he continued in his measured way, "and you will pardon me if the telling is long. Before it was my privilege to make your acquaintance I was not, as you know, a bachelor; my wife"—and he accentuated the possessive pronoun as had he had but one—"was to me very dear. When I lost her, I thought at first there was nothing left me, but with time I grew to believe that life might still be livable. It is easy for you to understand that in my misfortune I was not dogmatic. I knew that no one is perfect, and I felt that if my wife had seemed perfection to me it was because we understood and loved one another. Then, too, as years passed I found my solitude very tedious. I was, it is true, no longer young, but I was not what the world has agreed to call old; and I thought that among the gracious women whom I knew it might be possible for me to find one who would consent to dispel the solitude, and who might perhaps be able to bring me some semblance of my former happiness. It was under these conditions that I met you. You remember what followed. I saw that you were beautiful, more so, indeed, than my wife, and I imagined that you were honest and self-respecting—in fact, a girl destined to become a noble woman. It was then that I ventured to address you. You told me of your poverty; I begged you to share the money which was mine; you told me that you did not love me. I answered that I would wait. I was glad to share the money with you. I was willing to wait. I knew that you would adorn riches; I believed that I could win your love, and I felt that the winning would be pleasant. I even admired you for the agreement which you suggested. I thought it could not come from any one not wholly refined and mistress of herself. In short, believing in your frankness, I offered you what I had to give. In return what did I ask? The opportunity to be with you, the opportunity of winning your affection and therewith a little trust, a little confidence and the proper keeping of my name. Surely I was not extravagant in my demands. And you, for all your frankness, omitted to tell me the one thing essential: you omitted to tell me—"

"Do not say it," the girl wailed; "do not say it." The tears were falling, her form was rocked with sobs. She was piteous before him who knew not what pity was.

He had risen and she crouched as though she feared he had risen to strike her.

"Of your lover whom I caught to-night cheating at cards."

He had struck her indeed. She looked up through her tears astonished at the novelty of the blow, and yet still she did not seem to understand. She stared at him vacantly as though uncertain of the import of his words.

"Of your lover," he repeated; "the blackleg."

She rose from her seat. She was trembling from head to foot. To support herself she stretched a hand to the mantel and clutching it, she steadied herself. Then, still looking him in the face, she said huskily, "You tell me Lenox Leigh cheated at cards? It is not true!"

"He *is* your lover, then!" hissed Incoul, and into his green, dilated eyes there came a look of such hideous hate that the girl shrank back.

In her fear she held out her arms as though to shield herself from him, and screamed aloud. "You are going to kill me!" she cried.

"Be quiet," he answered, "you will wake the house."

But the order was needless. The girl fell backwards on the lounge. He stood and looked at her without moving. Presently she moaned; her eyes opened and her sobs broke out afresh. And still he gazed as though in the enjoyment of a hope fulfilled.

"Now get to your bed," he said, at last.

His eyes searched the room. On a table was a pink box labeled bromide of potassium, and filled with powders wrapped in tin foil. He opened and smelled of one and then opened another and poured the contents of both into a glass which he half filled with water.

"Drink it," he said.

She obeyed dumbly. The tears fell into the glass as she drank. But in a little while her sobs came only intermittently. "I will sleep now," she murmured, helplessly. "I think I will sleep now." Yet still he waited. Her head had fallen far back on the sofa, her hair drooped about her shoulders, her lips were gray.

He took her in his arms and carried her to the bed. One of her furred slippers dropped on the way, the other he took from her. The foot it held hardly filled his palm. He loosened her gown. He would have taken it off but he feared to awake her. Was she really asleep, he wondered. He peered down at her eyelids but they did not move. Surely she slept. A door that led to a dressing-room was open. He closed it. The chair in which he had sat he restored to its original position. Then he turned out the gas. On each of the fixtures his fingers rested the fraction of a minute longer than was necessary. He groped to the door, opened it noiselessly and listened. There was no sound. The house was still as a tomb. He closed the door behind him and drawing the nameless instrument from his pocket he inserted it carefully in the keyhole, gave it a quick turn and went to his room.

CHAPTER XVIII.
MR. INCOUL GOES OVER THE ACCOUNTS.

There is a saying to the effect that any one who walks long enough in front of the Grand Hôtel will, in the course of time, encounter all his acquaintances, past, present and to be. On the second day after the dinner in the Parc Monceau, Mr. Blydenburg crossed the boulevard. It was an unpleasant afternoon of the kind which is frequent in the early winter: the air was damp and penetrating, and the sky presented that unrelieved and cheerless pallor of which Paris is believed to be the unique possessor. Mr. Blydenburg's spirits were affected; he was ill at ease and inclined to attribute his depression to the rawness of the air and the blanched sky above him. He was to leave Paris on the morrow, and he felt that he would be glad to shake its mud from his feet. He was then on the way to his banker's to close an account, and as he trudged along, with an umbrella under his arm and his trousers turned up, in spite of the prospect of departure he was not in a contented or satisfied frame of mind.

For many hours previous he had cross-questioned himself in regard to Incoul. He knew that in speaking out his mind he had done right, yet he could not help perceiving that right-doing and outspokenness are not always synonymous with the best breeding. Truth certainly is attractive, particularly to him who tells it, but one has to be hospitably inclined to receive it at all times as a welcome guest. Beside, he told himself, Incoul was a man to whom remonstrance was irksome, he chafed at it no matter what its supporting truths might be. Perhaps then it would have been better had he held his tongue. Incoul was his oldest friend, he could not afford to lose him; at his time of life the making of new ones was difficult. And yet did he seek him in a conciliatory mood it would be tantamount to acknowledging that Incoul had been in the right, and the more he thought the matter over the more convinced he became that Incoul was in the wrong. Leigh, he could have sworn, was innocent. The charge that had been brought against him was enough to make a mad dog blush. It was preposterous on the face of it. Then, too, the young man had been given no opportunity to defend himself. The honest-hearted gentleman did not make it plain to his own mind how Leigh could have defended himself even had the opportunity been offered, but he waived objections; his faith was firm. He was enough of a logician to understand that circumstantial evidence, however strong, is not unrebuttable proof, and he assured himself, unless the young man confessed his guilt, that he at least would never believe it.

He was not, therefore, in a contented or satisfied frame of mind; he was irresolute how to act to Incoul; he did not wish to lose an old friend and he was physically unable to be unjust to a new one. After crossing the boulevard he passed the Grand Hôtel and just as he left the wide portals behind him he saw Mr. Wainwaring with whom two days before he had dined in the Parc Monceau. He bowed and would have continued his way, but Mr. Wainwaring stopped him.

"You have heard, have you not?" he asked excitedly, "you have heard about Mrs. Incoul?"

"Heard what?"

"It appears that on going to bed on Sunday night she turned the gas on instead of turning it off. They smelled the gas in the hall and tried to get into the room, but the door was locked; finally they broke it down. They found her unconscious though still breathing; they worked over her for five hours, but it was no use."

Blydenburg grounded his umbrella on the pavement for support. "Good God!" he muttered. "Good God!"

"Yes," Mr. Wainwaring continued, "it is terrible! A sweeter girl never lived. My daughter knew her intimately; she went there this morning to see her and learned of it at the door. I have just been up there myself. I thought Incoul might see me, but he couldn't. Utterly prostrated I suppose. I can understand that. We all know how devoted he was. He will never get over it—never."

Blydenburg still held to his umbrella for support.

"I must go there," he said.

"Yes, go by all means; he will see you, of course. Poor Incoul! I am heartily sorry for him. After all, wealth is not happiness, is it?"

At this platitude Blydenburg would have gone, but Mr. Wainwaring had more news to impart. "You know about young Leigh, Mrs. Manhattan's brother, don't you?" he continued.

Blydenburg looked down at his umbrella in a weary way.

"Yes, I was there," he answered, "but I don't believe it."

"Oh, you mean that affair at the club. Well, it appears that it is true. From what I make out of the papers, he went to his hotel afterwards, and took a dose of morphine. It was his only way out of it. I couldn't bear him, could you?"

Blydenburg nodded vacantly. "He must have been guilty."

"As to that there is no doubt. De la Dèche says it is a wonder he was not caught before. Well, good day; tell Incoul how profoundly grieved we all are. Good day."

Presently Blydenburg found himself in a cab. He was a trifle dazed at what he had heard. He was not brilliant; he was very tiresome at times, the sort of a man that likes big words and small dictionaries, yet somehow he was lovable and more human than many far cleverer than he. To his own misfortune he had a heart, and in disasters like these it bled. He would have crossed the Continent to bring a moment's pleasure to the girl that had been asphyxiated in her bed, and he would have given his daughter to the man who had been choked down to the grave. Then, too, as nearly as he could see, he had wronged Incoul and Incoul was in great grief. As the Urbaine rolled on, his thoughts did not grow nimbler. In his head was a full, aching sensation; he felt benumbed, and raised the collar of his coat. Soon the cab stopped before the house in the Parc Monceau. He had no little set speech prepared; he wanted merely to take his friend by the hand and let him feel his sympathy unspoken, but when the footman came in answer to his ring, he was told that Mr. Incoul could see no one. He went back to his cab. It had begun to rain, but he did not notice it, and left the window open.

As the cab rolled down the street again, Mr. Incoul, who had been occupied with the morning paper, sent for the courier.

"Karl," he said, when the man appeared, "I will go over your accounts."

THE END.

Milton Keynes UK
Ingram Content Group UK Ltd.
UKHW011124180424
441376UK00004B/195

9 789357 951265